VAUGHN: FIREBRAND COWBOYS

BARB HAN

TORJAKE PUBLISHING

Copyright © 2023 by Barb Han

All rights reserved.

No part of this book may be reproduced in any form or by any electronic or mechanical means, including information storage and retrieval systems, without written permission from the author, except for the use of brief quotations in a book review.

Editing: Ali Williams

Cover Design: Jacob's Cover Designs

Please be aware that there are references to previous childhood physical abuse. I hope I have dealt with these issues as they and you deserve.

To my family for being the great loves of my life.

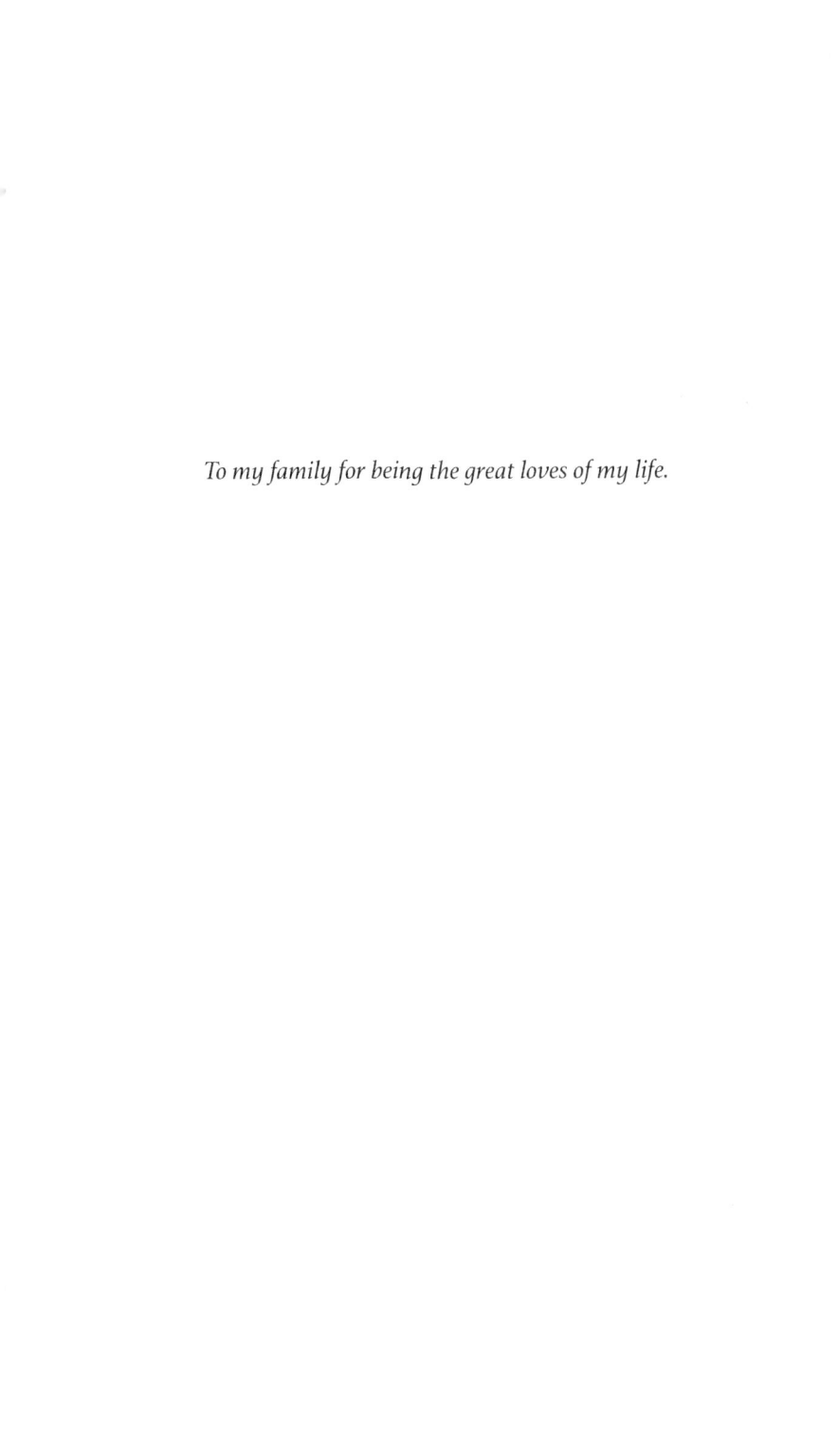

1

Getting shot sucked.

Vaughn Firebrand could attest to the fact, and he didn't recommend it. A bullet fragment had taken a small chunk of skin out of his thigh, which still hurt like hell. He would like to say that his week had gotten better from there. However, rolling down a Colorado mountain in a minivan after being shot at—again—didn't exactly qualify as an improvement.

Move, dammit. Open your eyes.

After counting to ten, Vaughn had lost count of how many times the vehicle had rolled. So, he could add banging his head, airbag deployment burns, and a headache like nobody's business to his list of 'things he'd rather not repeat.' Not to mention the fact he'd been unconscious for a time.

Shake it off or get shot again.

The sobering thought kicked his butt in gear. He blinked, and then forced his eyes to stay open. It took a few seconds to get his bearings and push through the fog wrapping around his brain like octopus tentacles. Vaughn released a string of swear words that would make his grandmother blush the second he realized the passenger door was open, the seat empty. Katy Castillo was gone.

The whole scenario came rushing back to him. There'd been a shooter chasing him from halfway up the mountain. The minivan he was driving had taken a couple of survivable hits. But it was the second vehicle coming at him head-on that had caused him to recalculate his odds of staying alive, which led to a risky move.

Taking a chance on rolling the vehicle over the side of the mountain where there was no guardrail had been the better of two bad options. Being in a gunfire sandwich didn't make for good survival odds.

With the sun descending behind the mountains, it would be black as pitch out here soon. He needed to find Katy and get her to safety before whoever had been shooting at them did.

After taking a quick inventory on his body parts—and deciding for better or worse they were all there—Vaughn attempted to open his door. He couldn't see out of the driver's side window, which meant he was up against the mountain or a tree. Tree, he decided. It had to be since the minivan couldn't be tipped on its side, considering the passenger door was wide open. It would have shut otherwise. Katy would have had to climb out the sliding door in the back.

He listened for any sign she might still be around. Nothing but nature, and nothing reassuring.

The whole ordeal with her politician uncle, Blaine Cargill, was supposed to be over. She was supposed to be out of danger. The Raker brothers were in jail for attempted kidnapping, among a host of other charges; they'd been trying to use Katy as leverage against the man who had been like a second father to her, to gain his cooperation to sell protected land for development.

Vaughn threw his shoulder into the door as he pulled the handle one more time. The only response was a sharp pain shooting down his arm. He craned his neck around, fighting off the pain that was almost blinding. It was the sharp kind that made him think that stabbing himself with a needle would be a welcome distraction.

Rather than continuing to do the same thing over and over again with the same result, he unhooked his seatbelt, climbed over the passenger seat, and exited through the opened door. There was something about the path of least resistance that was a beautiful thing, though even movement took a lot of effort. His strength was roughly sixty percent right now, which had gotten him through a lot of physical fights but wouldn't cut it while trying to outrun a bullet.

Katy's handbag was missing, so she must have had the presence of mind to take it with her. He tried not to be too offended she'd left him an unconscious sitting duck. There could be another explanation for her absence, like one of the shooters found what they were looking for and dragged her out of the vehicle.

Voices echoed, and he knew there was a good chance the bastards weren't giving up. What did he expect? They wouldn't carefully track him, shoot up his vehicle, and then just assume he was dead when he rolled the minivan off the mountain. No, that would be too easy. Assassins, trained killers—whatever name he slapped on them—didn't leave anything to chance. He wouldn't, either. His military training had taught him to dot every i and cross every t on a mission. Vaughn bit back a curse as he limped along, grabbing onto tree trunks as he made his way down the mountain and toward the sound of rushing water.

His thigh felt like it was being stabbed with half a dozen splinters with every step. Before he got too far, he checked his jeans where the recent bullet fragment had entered. There was a dark spot flowering on the outside of his thigh. This wasn't what he needed. Cold, wet liquid trickled down his leg as his eyesight blurred. He must still be woozy from the forced accident. There wasn't enough blood loss to cause trouble. At least, he didn't think so.

A shadow covered more than half of the mountain now, the sun in full retreat.

He had to laugh at the irony of what would be considered a normal life versus his. A typical person was getting close to clocking out of work on a Friday afternoon, possibly ready to hit a happy hour to find a strong drink and a nice hookup. By contrast, he was bleeding out in a ravine on the side of a mountain in Colorado. If that didn't give an indication of how his life was going lately, he didn't know what would.

Oddly enough, he would normally feel like the winner in this equation. A 'normal' life had never been the goal. But lately his life was beginning to feel all adrenaline and no down time. Being a career soldier had its downsides.

His blood loss didn't get him too riled up at this point. He'd survived worse circumstances and come out on top. The problem was that it would leave a trail that could get him found and killed. The folks after him and Katy weren't shooting Nerf guns. They meant business, as evidenced by the fact they used real bullets and had come at them from front and back. Their tactical mission had one scope...erase them both.

Then there was the problem of him losing consciousness. Could it really have been for more than a minute or two? He had no recollection of Katy bolting out of the vehicle. Although, their history proved she kept her running shoes on in a tight situation. She'd hit pro-level there.

The two of them went all the way back to high school, which was the reason he'd agreed to protect her in the first place, after her uncle had first contacted Vaughn, pleading for his help. At one time, a very long time ago, he and Katy had been sweethearts. She'd bruised his ego and broken his heart in one fell swoop. Even though their breakup was a long time ago, the wounds were as raw as if they'd happened last week. Why?

Vaughn had been asking himself that question more years than he wanted to count. An answer had been as elusive as a Bigfoot sighting. Right now, though, he needed to refocus on getting out of the current situation in one piece.

At this point, it was anyone's guess as to which direction she would take to get away from the vehicle. He tried not to let his pride become too bruised at the fact she'd been a little too willing to abandon him while he'd been passed out and vulnerable. Of course, it might not have been her choice. That would be a whole new problem.

Assuming that she would be smart enough not to climb up toward the shooters, he decided that she would have headed down toward the water. Whether she would track east or west was anyone's guess.

He glanced around and then made sure he had his cell phone before he got too far away. He could call her. Unless he'd missed something back at the minivan, she'd taken her handbag with her. Vaughn fished his cell out of his pocket as he methodically made his way down the mountain. Out here, he probably wouldn't have any bars, but it was worth a shot. How easy would it be if he could just give Katy a call and ask for her location? Too easy. Way too easy. In Vaughn's life, Lady Luck wasn't someone who smiled on him a whole lot. She was shy and rarely visited, which had caused him to work hard rather than rely on chance.

Vaughn dimmed the light on his screen so that he didn't turn into a beacon for the bastards who were chasing him and Katy. He checked for bars. Just as suspected, there were none. He fired off a text to his cousin Hudson anyway, figuring the second Vaughn got coverage, the message would go through and he wouldn't have to babysit his phone. He'd sent an earlier message about needing to take care of something before coming home. That 'something' was lost at present.

Taking a chance, he headed east. He'd mistakenly assumed leaving Texas would be all it would take to protect Katy until the dust settled after the Raker brothers' arrests. The plan had been to secure her at his buddy's fishing cabin while Vaughn headed into town to keep watch. He'd intended to make sure no one decided to attempt to drive up the path that led to his buddy's place by parking himself at the base. Everything about this mission had gone FUBAR, and this was supposed to be the easy part.

The temptation to call out Katy's name was real, even if it meant whispering. The sun had slid behind the mountains, plunging him into complete darkness. Desperation was also real. Had he gone the wrong direction?

KATY CASTILLO DIMMED the screen on her cell phone. She'd been searching for bars now for a solid fifteen minutes, maybe longer. Circling back to the minivan, she couldn't risk staying away any longer.

After engaging in a death roll in the vehicle, her head felt like she'd just gotten off one of those spinning rides at the state fair. The kind famous for bringing up all the fun fried foods being sold.

Right now, her biggest concern was trying to get Vaughn out. She sent up a prayer that he was conscious. Seeing him with his head limp to one side had sent a panic attack rippling through her. There was no way she could dead lift him or drag him from the driver's seat while the door was jammed up against a tree. Trying to drag him across the console and passenger seat while the men shooting at them were still in the area hadn't seemed like the best plan.

She'd been praying for bars, knowing full well the idea was the equivalent of a 'Hail Mary' pass in football as time ran out. Since she couldn't find any, and it was dark outside, circling back was the only option.

Katy turned around and started the climb uphill. Male voices echoed, making it difficult to pinpoint the location of the source. From the sounds, they could be right on top of her. Icy fingers closed around her spine, sending a chill racing down her back as she retraced her steps. The only other noise was the chirp of insects and the occasional twig snapping nearby, which scared the bejesus out of her. This seemed like a good time to remind herself this area was known for deer. There were other scarier animals out there, sure, but she didn't want to think about bears and coyotes right now.

Pulling herself up the steep incline, one tree trunk at a time, she should be close to the vehicle. It was too dark to see her hand in front of her face at this point. Her eyes were slowly adjusting, not fast enough to get her bearings. Could she use her phone light to guide her?

The move would be risky. The voices had silenced, which might not mean anything. At least when she heard them, she knew they were in the general area. The echo meant they could be close, but they weren't right on top of her.

And Vaughn might be a sitting duck in the minivan. The thought braided her stomach lining. She had to get back to him before they did and figure out a Plan B for how to get him safely out of there.

Another wave of panic struck, hitting the center of her chest this time with the force of a lightning bolt. Her plan would have been great if it had worked. Leaving Vaughn unconscious with no way to defend himself to find nonexistent bars felt like she'd abandoned him and left him for dead.

Branches slapped her face and chest. The toe of her ballet flat tangled in scrub brush, nearly causing her to face plant. She threw her arms out in front of her. Her cell went flying. A crack sounded. *Please no. Not my cell.* She wouldn't last five minutes without it despite the fact there was no cell coverage to be found so far.

Katy dropped down on all fours, feeling around for her tech device. The sharp end of a stick poked her right palm. *Ouch.* She withdrew her hand and brought it to her mouth. Lot of good the move did.

At least her eyes were beginning to adjust as she frantically searched for her link to the outside world. She might not have bars in this exact location but she wouldn't give up hope this soon. She would find reception and call for help.

She listened. The same sounds filled the air, crickets and critters but no male voices. It was too much to hope they'd given up. No, Katy suspected these folks were trained to kidnap, kill, or both, which brought her back to her politician uncle's recent scandal. Considering the Raker brothers had been arrested, who else could have been involved in the scheme? Her uncle sure wasn't talking, but he had to have known other criminals were in the deal. Did he believe arrests would scare the others into retreating?

Did these possible others who might be involved in the deal believe she knew all the details? Because she could sit them down right now and set the record straight. Katy had no knowledge of the deal that had been going down, other than the Raker's participation. She'd believed they were the only source behind the blackmail attempt. She owed her uncle a visit to find out if anyone else could be involved. The conversation they needed to have would play out better in person. The questions she wanted to ask were mounting. But at this rate, she might not make it off this mountain alive.

Feeling around, frustration mounted as she searched for her cell. The cold, hard earth punished her knees as she crawled around. There was no way she could be without her lifeline to the world. She got anxious feelings just thinking about losing her connection to the outside world. It was wild just how dependent she'd become on the piece of technology.

Please, please, give me just one break today.

Katy blew out a frustrated breath as she came up empty on the cell search. The trail back to the minivan was lost. Her cell was lost. *She* was lost. Something wet touched her hand as she raked it across the ground. She immediately pulled it back as though it had been bit. A dozen fire ants crawled on her skin, or at least that's the way it felt. On closer inspection, she realized the offending object was moss on a rock.

She realized she was being overly dramatic but there was something extra scary about being lost in the woods at night, not to mention there were men with guns searching for her.

Being from Texas, most would assume she'd grown up camping in the outdoors, and that she could shoot a gun. She had news for folks. The outdoors might be for hunting and fishing, but she participated in neither.

A noise sounded to her left. She suppressed a gasp. A few seconds ticked by without another sound other than her frantic heartbeat.

Dammit, these jerks didn't get to win. Not today. More of that frustration engulfed her, turning into a burning fire in her belly. They might kill her, but she had no intention of going down easy. Determination replaced fear.

Running her hand along the ground, her fingers stopped on a familiar object. She grabbed her cell and held it tight to her chest, thankful for this one break.

One down. One to go.

The minivan should be close, according to her estimation. In fact, the marker of the fallen pine tree was right next to her. She climbed up a little higher and looked around. Her eyes were getting better but she wished she could use her cell phone to light her path. She didn't dare to turn it on though.

An unfamiliar male voice cut through the night a second before a hand closed around her mouth from behind.

2

"It's me," Vaughn whispered into Katy's ear a second after she bit the living daylights out of his hand. Every muscle in his body coiled to stop him from yelling in pain. She had the jaw strength of a pit bull.

She immediately turned around and wrapped her arms around his midsection, pulling him so close there wasn't an inch of space between them.

"I'm sorry," she said into his chest. It was hard to be mad at her while her body was flush with his. Besides, her voice had a way of piercing his armor. It always had, even back in high school when they'd been best friends before going official and deciding to stop fighting their attraction. Katy had been certain it would ruin their friendship, claiming that was the reason for her holdout. She'd said she couldn't stand the thought of losing him and then pointed out that high school relationships rarely went the distance.

He was still trying to figure out the real reason she'd changed her mind and been the one to end things, after what he'd believed had been two of the best years of his life. She'd been state fair memories of driving up to Dallas, just the two of them, and spending the day riding rides, playing games, and eating every new fried food on the menu. Fried butter? No, thanks.

Call it hurt pride or plain old bruised ego, but Vaughn needed to know why she'd crushed his heart before he could truly move on. He'd dated plenty of women in the past ten years, and not one measured up. It was high time he put the past behind him, and that had been the second part of this mission. The initial call from Katy's uncle had felt like a sign from the universe. Closure was within reach.

"Here it is," one of the male voices said. He wasn't more than twenty feet away from Vaughn and Katy, shining a light on the minivan. His back was to them, so Vaughn couldn't get a good look. He was tempted to pull out his own cell phone and snap a picture but they were too close. He couldn't risk the flash. "Well, hell, it's empty."

There wasn't much in the way of protection where he and Katy stood, so he quietly pulled her behind a solid tree trunk.

"They couldn't have gone too far," a second voice surmised.

"Nope," the voice said. It was impossible to get a visual on their faces. "How much you want to bet they're lying around here somewhere."

A sweep of light moved across the area. Katy sucked in a breath and he could feel her heart racing in her chest. Pride he shouldn't allow filled his chest at the fact she was holding it together. Katy had always been calm under pressure in high school. It was comforting to know that not everything had changed about her in the past ten years.

He reached for her hand and gave a squeeze of reassurance. The jolt of lightning that came with skin-to-skin contact was nothing more than muscle memory from an attraction that hadn't dimmed. Then again, being physically attracted to her wasn't the problem. Katy was five-feet-ten-inches of mostly legs. She had blonde hair that had been almost platinum growing up, thanks to her Swedish roots, with eyes the rarest shade of blue that were like looking into glass pools. She could have been related to Tiger Woods' ex-wife Elin Nordegren for how much the two resembled each other. In fact, he was pretty sure there was a second or third cousin/distant relative connection between the two.

Katy could have walked a runway if she'd wanted to but being in the spotlight didn't interest her one bit. She'd been shy and quiet, until he really got to know her. Another side of her personality was revealed to the precious few she trusted enough to let inside her inner circle. Maybe that was the reason he'd felt special? Lots of kids wanted to be friends with her but she chose the people closest to her carefully. Not in a way that came across as being stuck up. She'd been nice to everyone. It was her nature to be reserved. So, he'd mistaken her interest in him and their relationship as something real. How special could he have been if it had been so easy to throw what they had away?

"Probably dead," Voice One said.

"We can't take a chance like that," Voice Two warned. "R.S. wants a body."

"No witnesses and no ties back to him," Voice One said. "I know. But how did we pull this crap assignment? Chasing down a senator's niece who is running with ex military sounds like a date with a jail cell."

"We don't pick 'em," Voice Two agreed. "But we don't renege, either. Boss man wants her dead. She's dead."

"Hard to kill one of our own, though," Voice Two said. He must be talking about military experience.

"It's either him or us," Voice One said.

"We have to find him first," Voice Two pointed out. Under normal circumstances, Vaughn wouldn't mind the odds with these two. However, he wasn't at full strength. Plus, he had Katy with him. He couldn't risk anything happening to her. Retreat was the only option until he could regroup and track those bastards down.

Vaughn memorized the initials R.S., figuring this was the person pulling the strings on the operation. They must have a tie to the Raker brothers, so digging around in Austin would be next. *If* he could get them off this mountain in one piece.

"That bitch is more trouble than she's worth," Voice One bit out. At sixty percent strength, there was no way Vaughn could risk taking on Voice One and Voice Two, not at the same time.

He bit back a curse, wanting nothing more than to shove the derogative word down Voice One's throat.

"Look at this," Voice One said.

"What?" Voice Two asked. They were walking around, no doubt trying to find a trail to follow.

"Blood," Voice One said. "We hit one of them."

"Or both. Told you they couldn't be far," Voice Two said. "No one could survive driving off a mountain. Not for long and not without help."

How the hell was Vaughn supposed to get Katy out of here now that the pair of men were on to something? How long before Voice One and Voice Two caught up to them?

"There ain't no one else around for miles, including the law," Voice One said, revealing a slight drawl to his voice. His accent was south Texas. The other one had a slightly Cajun twang. Vaughn took note of both as he drew Katy closer to him. Footsteps moved down the mountain, following a path that would lead the men right back here.

Could Vaughn get to his weapon before they returned and then pick them off one by one? It might be the only chance they had to escape. He was slower than usual and Katy had no idea what she was up against. It was probably better that way, too. As it was, her pulse pounded so hard it almost felt like her heart might burst through her ribs.

As the pair of men followed Vaughn's blood trail, he inched around the tree, using it to shield them from view.

It would take the men several minutes to work their way back up the mountain as he had. Vaughn had returned in the hopes of getting to his weapon. In his earlier fog, he'd forgotten it, thinking a spare had been strapped to his ankle. It was a mistake he might have paid a high price for.

As the footsteps moved down into the distance, he mentally calculated the number of steps it would take to get to his Sig Sauer. At twenty feet from the minivan, he could make it there in eight strides. Of course, he'd have to go in through the passenger door. Since the men left well enough alone, it shouldn't be a problem getting into the vehicle with the door already open. The light dimmer either wasn't working or the timer cut it off.

Since the pair of men coming for them were ex-military, Vaughn had a sense of the way they would think. Based on the blood and the crash, it was logical to believe Vaughn and Katy might be lying in the ravine, bleeding out. His instincts would have him searching for a water source for survival, especially if he was mortally injured. It was unknown which one of them was hit and optimistic to believe both had been. Then again, he always calculated the worst-case scenario and worked based on it.

The bastards had a ton of firepower and weren't afraid to shoot out here. Gunfire would echo, much like the voices. Meaning, there would be emergency vehicles showing up at some point. Someone had to live here even if it was just a random cabin here or there. Folks who chose a life on a mountain with very few, if any, neighbors would have their own weapons and be ready to use them.

Whoever this R.S. person was, needed to be found and exposed. The man had been willing to kill women and children, proving he didn't deserve the freedoms Vaughn and his unit had put their lives on the line to protect. Case in point, this R.S. person had recently targeted an innocent pregnant woman on his path to locating Katy. He'd planned to use her as a bargaining chip against her uncle and proved he would erase anyone who got in his way accidentally or otherwise. The man had shown his true colors and his ruthlessness. Vaughn had had no choice but to turn the pregnant Anisa Turner over to his cousin Hudson, who'd managed to keep her safe until the Raker brothers could be caught and fell in love in the process.

The arrests were supposed to signal the end of Katy's nightmare. The trip to Colorado had been supposed to be a precaution. Instead of providing a safe haven, he was on a mountain with a woman who might run away and abandon him if he turned his back for two seconds.

KATY FELT the moment Vaughn's muscles coiled and couldn't help but wonder why. He'd been quiet, so she assumed he was assessing the situation, figuring out a next move that would keep them both alive. Meanwhile, she'd been fixated on the mention of blood. Was Vaughn hurt?

Since she couldn't ask or see well enough in the dark to assess any possible wounds for herself, she filed the thought away for future use.

"Stick close to me," Vaughn finally whispered, when it was clear the pair of men were long gone. She figured they must be following his blood trail, meaning he would know exactly where that would lead and how long it would take them to return. "Be glue."

She nodded, unsure why considering she was behind him. A quick squeeze of his hand conveyed the message. He moved, keeping her tight to his back until they reached the passenger side of the minivan.

The most she could do was keep watch while he climbed over the seat with a small grunt. It told her that he was in pain, which meant he was shot in addition to his bruises from the accident. How she'd gotten away without any major injuries was a miracle she decided not to question. At this point, she was grateful to the person who invented airbags. Without them, there was no way either of them would have survived, let alone walked away with only a few minor bruises. Her shoulder hurt when she lifted her arm, so she assumed she'd taken a little damage. Nothing compared to what it could have been.

Keeping watch when a blanket of darkness covered the area was as productive as throwing a bucket of water on a raging wildfire. But she did her best to track anything that moved.

Considering this area was covered in pine trees, the moonlight couldn't break through enough to give her anything to work with. The light on her cell was useless to her right now. While she waited, she considered the initials R.S.

This person wanted to erase her existence enough to send ex-military men after her, to make sure the job was done right. One trained assassin wasn't exactly someone she wanted coming after her, let alone two. Fear gripped her at the thought someone was trying to kill her. Panic robbed her voice. Anger slowly boiled the blood in her veins. This wasn't supposed to be her life. Traipsing through trees while trying to steady her breathing so she didn't have a full-on panic attack wasn't high on her to-do list. Her footsteps were heavy no matter how hard she tried to lighten them.

Vaughn moved like a panther, quiet and deadly. He retrieved something from underneath the seat on the driver's side. Metal glinted against what little light crept through the trees where they stood.

As his hand found hers again, a bright light blinded her.

"Got you, sonofabitch," a third voice said, sending ice water running down her back.

The light was to their left, burning her retinas to the point she put her hand up to block. Before she could process what was happening enough to act, she was being moved behind the opened minivan door.

The crack of a bullet split the air. The pair of voices from earlier cursed as she heard the men doubling back. Time froze.

Vaughn was gone in the next second, rolling out of the view of the light. A flash in the darkness was followed by the crack sound. This time, it was Vaughn firing. The light dropped onto the ground.

"You shot me," the third voice said. He sounded pissed off more than anything else. Katy wondered where he'd taken the hit if he could be so calm. An arm? A shoulder? Couldn't have been anywhere fatal. Right? She remembered being told real life wasn't like the shows on TV. When someone was shot, it took a minute for their brain to catch up to the news, which was why they didn't immediately drop.

The cell light was smothered by scrub brush, so it didn't

help with visibility. She strained to get a look, but came up empty.

Vaughn fired a couple more shots before he was suddenly at her side again, urging her to move in the opposite direction of the shooter and away from the passenger door. Heavy footsteps sounded a little too close for comfort. Hers were the equivalent of an elephant running through trees, whereas Vaughn was as quiet as a church mouse. How?

Clearly the man's military training had kicked in and, from the looks of it, he was one of the best. Then again, he'd had more than a decade to sharpen his skills in battle.

"I'm going after the others," he said to her in barely more than a whisper. Even now, after all these years, his deep timbre sent sensitized shivers racing across her skin and an electrical current charging through her. "I need you to stay low and stay put. Okay?"

"Yes," she confirmed. He was the expert here. She wouldn't challenge his judgment, no matter how freaked out she was at the thought of being alone out here with two gunmen within range.

Vaughn disappeared into the darkness. She crouched down and felt around for anything she could use as a weapon. Her fingers landed on a stick, which couldn't hurt to have on hand. She also located a palm-sized rock with a jagged edge. Definitely a better choice, if push came to shove.

It was shocking how quiet Vaughn could be out here. Her respect for him doubled as she thought about what a mess she would be without him. Funnily enough, he'd had to talk her into letting him take her to his buddy's cabin. After the arrests, she'd been naïve enough to think the whole ordeal was over. She'd even used the word *overkill* to describe his idea.

The next time she decided to put up an argument against Vaughn, she made a note to think twice. Him showing up in her life again made her second guess another decision she'd made in the past. But she'd had no choice. And just because the man was six-feet-four-inches of muscle and pure sex appeal, didn't mean she could let her attraction to him get out of control again. With hair as black as the velvet sky and striking blue eyes she could stare into for days, it was easy to get lost in him.

Minutes had ticked by with no sounds, no word. And then something moved.

3

Vaughn circled around behind the pair of men. He could probably fire off a shot and nail one of the bastards without much fanfare. Getting the second one would prove trickier. Their weapons were out, and ready. He would miss critical seconds, which could get him shot.

Getting shot was no fun. Repeat. No fun. Those words were becoming his mantra.

Tracking them a little farther, he realized they'd gone off the trail. Vaughn bit back a curse. They were moving him away from the minivan on purpose. He was being led somewhere by folks who thought like him. They would realize he'd tucked Katy away somewhere because it would be easier and quieter to move without her. She was a civilian and, therefore, terrible at this game.

And then he heard one set of footsteps. The men had split up. Hell's bells. This was just his luck lately. To get cocky enough to believe he could outsmart these two. Underestimating them was a critical mistake. Sure, his IQ had been noted on his chart. It was decent. It also worked against him in this case because he'd read these two at face value.

So, he gave credit where it was due.

Turning back to where Katy was hiding might lead them straight to her. Was it worth the risk? Leaving her exposed and vulnerable wasn't the play. She didn't have a weapon. It was dark, but these guys weren't afraid to use the flashlight app on their phones. Then again, they'd had a secret weapon earlier. A third man who was being quiet.

In fact, when he really thought about it, their plan had been spot-on so far. Two of them had made noise at the minivan, while the third lurked in the shadows. Vaughn suddenly remembered hearing three voices earlier, but it had been easy to forget about the third. Most three-person teams would have one of the players hang back at the vehicles to make sure the law didn't catch on or some random driver didn't show up. With a couple of cars parked on the side of the road, a good Samaritan would stop to see if more assistance was needed, which might cast suspicion on the situation and a call to 911. A vehicle going over the side of the mountain wasn't exactly unexpected in these parts, so locals would stop to offer assistance. Folks who lived out here were much like ranchers. Learning to live off the land and survive in severe and unpredictable conditions caused folks to take care of their neighbors.

Bringing him back to his point about the third voice. He'd slipped under Vaughn's radar.

The sound of sirens echoed through the canyon, the first lucky break. Vaughn's thigh was on fire and he couldn't sustain standing up much longer. He needed to address his wound and get back to Katy.

Circling back, he found her exactly where he'd left her. There were no sounds of footsteps any longer, a sure sign these guys were taking no chances on getting caught. It also reminded Vaughn they'd been deliberate with their noises earlier. The mistake was on him.

The second Katy saw him, she came flying out of the brush and launched herself at him.

"What happened?" he asked instinctively.

"Someone was here," she said. "He was so close that I thought it was over. There was no way he wasn't going to find me. And then the siren sounded. He took off." She sniffed before ducking her head, as though she didn't want him to see her overcome with emotion.

"I'm here now," he reassured. "And we have to go."

"Where?" she asked with traces of shock in her voice.

"Away from here," he said, taking her by the hand and then linking their fingers. He moved west this time, the opposite direction from home. And he climbed up instead of going down to the ravine. It was counterintuitive for survival purposes, but down was exactly where the other two would go. They would follow the water source down to a town, and then probably steal a vehicle to get across state lines. If he had to guess, they'd look for a street-legal motorcycle in someone's garage. This time of year, the owner might not realize it was gone for days, possibly a week, since the warmer summer months were long gone.

When they were far enough away for Vaughn to feel reasonably safe, he stopped and sat on a downed tree trunk. He would ask Katy how she was doing but her state of mind was pretty obvious at this point. She was keeping it under control and that was the most he could hope for under the circumstances.

"I've been racking my brain with the initials R.S.," she said, not wasting time. "They don't ring a bell."

"Once we can find cell coverage, a call to your uncle

might clear this up," he said, checking his thigh. He shrugged out of his sweater and then his undershirt. Cool air whipped around, bringing goosebumps to his skin's surface. He set the sweater down on the log, and gave a good shiver in the cold.

"You never could keep a shirt on," Katy said with a half-smile. There was a wistful quality to her tone that he didn't want to overanalyze. It was most likely nostalgia kicking in, now that they'd been around each other for a little while. Facing death also had a way of making folks think about the past and how fragile life could be.

"Nope," he admitted, figuring a little break in tension might be good for both of them. Besides, he needed a few minutes to process what had just happened. "And you used to tease me about it to no end."

She laughed. "Yep."

"In my defense, I was hot all the time," he said. "I did grow up in the Texas heat."

"Which didn't explain the need to keep your shirt off during winter months, especially calving season," she quipped. "Remember all those times I'd stop by and find you asleep while sitting up and half naked?"

He chuckled as he stood up and undid his belt buckle before unsnapping and unzipping his jeans. "How could I forget? You took pictures of me shirtless and freezing, and then sent them to me when I was trying to study for a test."

"I always put covers over you after, though," she defended. "And got underneath them to warm you up."

He didn't want to remember the good times with Katy, so he clamped his mouth shut. They didn't need to be chummy. The sweater came right back on before he got too cold. The jeans went down far enough for him to check the damage to his outer thigh now that his eyes had adjusted to the darkness.

She gasped when she got a good look. "How bad is it?" Then she added, "Be honest."

"It's more than a scratch but not as bad as a jugular vein being hit," he said.

"That's a pretty wide gap there," she pointed out. "Which is it closer to?"

"A bad scratch," he admitted.

A heavy sigh came next. "Since you downplay everything, I'll take it to mean this isn't good, but you're not going to bleed out on me."

Well, that really made him crack up. "I'll do my best."

"Good," she quipped. "Because I don't want to be stuck out here alone with no cell coverage." She broke into a smile that was the equivalent of a warm campfire on a cold night. Her sharp sense of humor was one of the many things he'd loved about her.

He cleared his throat and refocused. "Speaking of which, your uncle might be able to identify the person behind the initials if we can get bars."

"I had the exact same thought," she said, looking down at her feet. Her fingers twisted together like when she was nervous or out of her comfort zone.

Good. Neither one of them needed to get relaxed around each other again. The hollow ache in his chest returned, reminding him just how easy it had been for her to rip his heart out.

"What's the plan?" Katy asked, knowing Vaughn would have one. "To find cell coverage."

"I need to rest this leg before I can do anything else," he said as he wrapped his thigh with his undershirt, tying it off in a makeshift bandage after ripping it into strips. He winced as he tightened the knot and she realized he was in more pain than he wanted to admit.

"We need to set up camp if we're going to stick around," she reasoned, figuring it wouldn't hurt for her to get busy. Besides, sitting here, doing nothing, caused her mind to wander to places it probably didn't need to go. Worrying never fixed a problem. It only drained her energy. She wasn't getting caught in that spin cycle again.

Her mind immediately snapped to forbidden territory, Vaughn's mother. Katy was still unclear about why Jackie Firebrand had been arrested for attempted murder. Was the woman capable of such an act? On the one hand, Jackie had always been superficial but that didn't make her a killer.

Then again, there were pressing issues when it came to trying to stay alive long enough to eat their next meal let alone bring up a subject that would surely do nothing but cause Vaughn more pain. Being stuck out in the woods on a random mountain didn't seem like a good time to bring up uncomfortable topics even though she wanted to offer her sympathy. Vaughn might not have been close with his mother but she was awaiting trial in a case that had surely split his family into pieces. Katy had had terrible parents growing up, and yet this had to be a whole new level of hell.

Since this didn't seem like the right time to discuss his family, or anything else personal, she asked, "What can I gather up?"

He was already checking cell coverage on his dimmed screen. He shook his head and clamped his lips shut.

"We'll be hungry soon," he pointed out. She didn't think this was the time to tell him that her stomach felt empty already. So much so, that she'd eat a slab of beef if it were put in front of her right now, despite being a vegetarian. She occasionally ate fish, so, technically, she wasn't a diehard with her eating habits. The infrequent chicken sandwich made its way into her mouth. She must really be hungry to be thinking this much about food. So, yes, she would take pretty much anything right now without complaining. Except maybe insects. She drew the line there.

"We'll have to figure something out," she said, fresh out of ideas. There wasn't exactly a drive-through anywhere nearby and their vehicle wasn't drivable, so…

"I can set a trap," he said like it was the easiest thing in the world. "There's plenty to eat for you. Tree bark is good since it's cold outside. There's prickly pear cactus just about everywhere. The fruit is edible."

"I've walked into that hot mess," she said, twisting up her face to reflect her disapproval. "Spent an entire car ride picking needles out of my clothes and skin. They hurt like hell."

"Those can be tricky," he admitted. "Best to avoid that part."

"If you can," she said. There were other dangers out here. Her thoughts cycled back to the initials R.S. and who that could possibly be. The person was clearly connected to the Raker brothers. Law enforcement would be interested in this new development. Although, a lot of good they'd done in keeping her out of harm's way.

It was so frustrating to be stuck out here in the middle of nowhere when answers could literally be in the palm of her hand if she could just get some cell coverage. Then there were the three people who were after them…two now. It would be nice if they could circle back and get some identification off what she could only assume was a dead man of the third voice. Her body involuntarily shivered at the thought of someone being killed.

"Are you cold?" Vaughn immediately asked, as he kept his hand pressed to his bullet injury, no doubt to stem the bleeding. Once he got that under control, she prayed they could get going again. The thought of sleeping out here for an entire night, knowing full well the temperatures would plummet, wasn't something she wanted to contemplate. She'd heard about people staying warm—and therefore alive—using body heat. Being curled up next to her first love —and someone she couldn't have—for an entire night would be the worst kind of torture.

"Not really," she said. Thinking about the loss of life grounded her and brought tears to the backs of her eyes. There was always that tiny hope in her that people could change, make use of second chances. It hadn't really worked so well for her own parents, despite never wanting to give up on them. They'd been high school sweethearts who hadn't just grown out of love with each other, but seemed to actively hate one another by the time Katy entered high school. Their fights were so intense, she remembered hiding underneath her bed like a five-year-old afraid of monsters in the closet.

On the outside, her mother was a lawyer and her father an ER doctor. They looked like a respectable family. Behind closed doors, they did little more than argue. And after they'd had a couple of drinks to 'relieve pressure' from the day... Her father, Mark, had his own signature drink, the MarkRita. It was a margarita that was so strong, men twice his size remarked they could barely finish one.

Drinking was a problem to the degree that Katy rarely touched alcohol. Was her approach extreme? She could admit that it was. However, the last thing she wanted to do was follow in the footsteps of her parents.

The arguments about her had been the worst. She assumed her mother had had an affair since her so-called father called Katy a bastard when he wasn't aware she was listening. Of course, it was difficult not to hear when he was shouting despite her bedroom being on the second floor. Now that her parents were gone, killed two years ago in a single collision car accident, maybe she could ask her uncle if he knew who her real father was. Looking back, it was most likely the reason her uncle had always been so kind to her. His sister must have confided her secrets in him.

So, it seemed he could possibly clear up two question marks at one time.

Katy issued a sharp sigh. *If* she could locate a few bars and Voice One and Voice Two didn't find them first.

4

Fingers twisted together, Katy also chewed the inside of her cheek. Those were two big signs she was under duress. Who wouldn't be under the circumstances? And yet, he was beginning to be concerned about her stress levels.

"We don't have to hang out here for long," he finally said after studying her out of the corner of his eye. She needed to be on the move so she didn't feel stuck. Feeling stuck caused her to overthink a problem. It had been the reason she'd been a bad test taker in school. She got too inside her head and questioned what she knew. Actually, Katy had one of the sharpest minds of anyone he'd ever met. She also had dyslexia, which made reading slow going, and difficulty translating her ideas into words sometimes made it hard for her to express herself.

Vaughn remembered her being pulled out of class in grade school during certain subjects. Later on, she admitted to hating being put in a different reading group, one that was labeled as 'special.' She'd hated the term, stating there wasn't anything special about struggling to read when it seemed like it came naturally to everyone else. Hearing her say those words was one of many times he was reminded of the things he took for granted on a daily basis. All the letters stayed put on the page for him. Whereas hers moved around, and sometimes fell right off the page. Then, there were the color blocks she'd described. Blocks of colors that would cover words out of nowhere, making her eyes strain so hard to do what came easy to everyone else.

But he didn't want to feel sorry for the isolation she must have felt but never showed. Not right now.

Katy sat up a little straighter, and then got very still. She tilted her head to one side. "I hear something. Water?" She paused for a couple of beats. "Do you hear it?"

He strained to listen. "Could be."

Before he could push up to standing, she reached out and grabbed hold of his forearm.

"Stay here. I can check it out," she said. "It doesn't sound far."

"Stay in my sights, please," he said, retrieving his Sig and making certain it was ready to go. He might only have a second or two to respond. Normally, the barrel would point forward, but he wouldn't risk pointing it anywhere near Katy while she walked away.

Katy nodded before heading in the direction of the sound. She stopped after a couple of steps. "What are the chances those men came this way? Like, give me odds."

"I'd say fifty-fifty," he admitted, not liking those one bit. But being dishonest or downplaying the threat wouldn't do either of them any favors. She needed to know what she might be up against. "I'm an excellent shot but I need you to dive far out of the way if someone shows. Okay?"

"Hit the dirt," she said in agreement. "Haven't played that game since I was a kid." Her face twisted in worry. "Guess we'll see if I'm still good at it."

"Let's hope it doesn't come to that," he said more for himself than anything else despite being an excellent marksman.

"Right," she said before following the sound into the darkness. Her footsteps were loud, at least to the trained ear. Since the bastards after them were ex-military, like him, they would hear her coming from a mile away. As unsettling as the thought was, he was pinning all his hopes on the two of them going downstream to find a village. The vehicles parked on the roadway would not be able to be traced back to their source. He would bet money on the fact. Since there was a dead body near a minivan that couldn't be traced back to him, he couldn't exactly surrender to the law without being suspicious. The whole scene was suspect. Besides, if this R.S. was powerful enough to get a politician in his pocket, he might have connections in law enforcement too. In fact, it was almost a guarantee. These three were brazen, blocking him on the mountain road. There was enough isolation out here to be able to drive for a while without seeing any other vehicles, but the road wasn't completely deserted. The men had taken risks.

Despite Katy's promise to stay in his sights, she disappeared into the trees. His chest squeezed at the minute mark of losing visual on her. If another minute passed, he would go looking no matter how much his thigh burned. Speaking of which, he'd lost enough blood to be concerned if he had to run. Considering he'd left a good bit of it back at the crash site, he reminded himself to call Dagger, his tech buddy, and thank him for ensuring fingerprints, blood or any another DNA couldn't be tied back to him. Dagger's hacking skills were top-notch. Everyone needed a friend like him, especially in a world where it had become next to impossible to hide.

Katy's DNA was another story. She would have touched the seatbelt and the door handle. He could only hope she'd had the presence of mind to wipe down her prints, like he'd taught her when they first started this...this *mission*, for lack of a better word.

Now that they had a minute to get their bearings, he needed to ask just how much cleaning up they would need to do. Would it be the worst thing if she was tied to the crash site? He needed to think it through.

Her uncle would be notified immediately, which could bring more resources to them. Unless, of course, those resources were somehow tied to the mysterious R.S. There were also two men on the loose who didn't want to be caught, and a dead body. No matter what the reasoning, self-defense, tactical mission, being the one to pull the trigger never got easier on the conscience after the fact. No matter how righteous the kill, there was always guilt for taking a life. Vaughn had become an expert at compartmentalizing, figuring he'd deal with the emotional baggage in the future.

Was that his smartest move? He had no idea. It got him through the night and that was all that mattered in the present. As long as he stayed in the present, he would be fine. Or so the thinking went. He hoped it wouldn't come back to bite him in the backside one day.

A quick glance at the time on his cell phone had him standing up. Katy had been gone three minutes and that was two minutes too long. There hadn't been so much as a peep out of her. On balance, that was probably a good thing.

Except the men after them could sneak up on her and slip a hand over her mouth before she had a chance to scream.

Why had he let her go deeper into the thicket alone?

At this point, he was hopping on one leg due to the pain. There were supplies in the minivan, power bars and ibuprofen in the small emergency kit. There was drinking water. He wished he could go back and grab them. Although he didn't doubt they'd find something to eat tonight, even if there was no water until morning.

The chill in the air made him wish he could start a campfire. If they were going to spend the night on this mountain, they would have to use each other's bodies for heat. The feel of her silky skin was imprinted on his fingertips. The honey-like taste of her tongue when it delved into his, teasing him without mercy. The way her body molded to his all those times they'd curled up on the couch together. Those weren't images he needed to dwell on for his own sake.

Shifting gears, he refocused on getting them through the night. There could be a shelter around that would offer safety from wild animals. On second thought, it would be the first place authorities looked, not to mention a place Voice One and Two would scout. He didn't want himself or Katy to be identified with the scene of a murder.

They would have to set up camp.

Heavy footsteps sounded in front of him, deeper in the thicket. They could only belong to one person...Katy. Knowing she was safe and on her way back sent a rush of relief through him. In his weakened condition, he would struggle in a two-on-one fight. His Sig's nickname was Chaos. It seemed appropriate, considering the damage it could do. As long as he had Chaos, he had a decent shot of evening the odds.

As Katy emerged, a pair of eyes behind her glistened. They were too low to belong to humans. At its height, Katy was being stalked by a coyote or a mountain lion. Making noise might startle the animal away, but it could also draw unwanted attention. With a coyote, he needed to make himself known and stand his ground. A mountain lion required more of a delicate touch. Their powerful jaws could snap around a person's body, crushing bone.

He puts his hands up, palms out, in the surrender position. Katy made a face.

"Stay calm and keep walking toward me, slower," he instructed, looking right past her. "You don't want to eat either one of us, mountain lion. My meat would be too tough for you."

A look of fear crossed Katy's features but she followed directions. Vaughn wouldn't mind cooking up this guy. His stomach growled, picking that moment to put his hunger on display. As long as they didn't provoke this animal, they should be able to come out of this encounter in one piece. Two against one wasn't the kind of odds a mountain lion liked.

When Katy made it all the way to him, he tucked her behind his back. "Turn around and put your face toward it so you can show that you're not scared."

"But I am," she said as she followed his instructions once again. Now that she was safely tucked behind him, he slowly walked them back a couple of steps.

"You're good," he said in as calm a voice as he could manage. This wasn't his first wildlife encounter and it wouldn't be his last. He fully intended to go home after this, to Lone Star Pass, Texas, and the family's cattle ranch. His grandfather might have made a mess of things when he died and his mother might have become even greedier and gotten herself into trouble for it, but the land was his home. He'd been away long enough. It was time to make things right. Besides, recently seeing Hudson again reminded him there were a lot of good people in the family. Not everyone bickered and treated each other like crap. Plus, he had a few words for his brother Rafe.

The animal, whatever it was, stayed locked onto them. He couldn't shoot like he normally would if he was backed into a corner. Was there something else he could use to scare the dangerous cat away?

∼

KATY SQUATTED DOWN and picked up the jagged rock at her feet. Her eyes had long adjusted to the darkness, so at least she wasn't at a total disadvantage. She chunked the rock toward the pair of eyes staring at them from the thicket. And then she hissed at whatever stood behind those eyes.

Before Vaughn could get on her, the animal turned the opposite direction and then took off.

"That was a risky move," Vaughn said, his voice tight. His reaction caught her off guard, because she was proud of herself and thought he might feel the same. Didn't she just stop a wild animal from stalking them?

"It paid off," she defended with a little more ire in her voice than intended.

"Don't do anything like that ever again," he said harshly. Since he'd never been the type to think a woman couldn't do a job better than a man, she knew he wasn't being sexist. His reaction stung her pride. She thought she was doing the right thing. Helping after feeling helpless for this entire time.

"Excuse me for helping," she said, stepping away from him.

He stood there for a long moment, seething. She might still be able to read his mood, not that she would need to be able to right now, but she used to be able to tell what he was thinking. Not anymore. Now, she was just as clueless as the next guy as to what might be going on in his mind. It struck her as sad because they used to be able to finish each other's sentences. Twin flames, he'd called them. Years had passed, so she hadn't exactly expected to pick up where they'd left off. In fact, him showing up in her life at all had been the surprise of the decade. Katy had gone from job to job without much in the way of purpose. She'd gone from relationship to relationship without investing too much. Heaven forbid she end up like her parents. She still had recurring nightmares from their fights. They'd lost their lives drinking and arguing, despite being intelligent people who should have known better than to get behind the wheel drunk.

Emotions were like that...out of control. The minute someone fell in love, they lost their grip. And that scared the hell out of her because she'd been head over heels for Vaughn from the moment she met him. Holding a secret from him had been the worst of miseries because they'd always told each other everything.

The notion had been an innocent one. If they shared all their secrets, life would somehow magically work out. That wasn't how it worked in the real world; she'd learned the hard way. Some secrets were meant to stay buried. And she couldn't trust herself to be around him and keep a secret she so desperately had to.

Katy shook off the hand wrapping long, lean fingers around hers, squeezing the breath out of her. Keeping her emotions in check around Vaughn was proving more difficult than she expected. Should she be surprised? He'd been her first date, her first kiss, and her first love in every sense of the word.

She mentally shook off the moment that would lead her down a dark path. There was no use reliving a past she couldn't change. She'd seen firsthand how vitriol love could be and how much it could tear two people down. She'd experienced the backlash from anger that became a raging wildfire, destroying everything in its path.

"What do you propose we do next?" she finally asked, needing to pull her thoughts back to the present and away from the reason for the scars on her legs and torso. Therapy could only get her so far. She quit after being told to find forgiveness for her parents. They were gone and, frankly, she didn't see the point. Forgiving felt too much like letting them off the hook and she wasn't ready to take that step.

"I need a few minutes of shut eye," he said, surprising her with a softer tone after the last one had been sharp enough to slice bread. "Then, we can get on the move to find cell coverage."

"You don't want to reach out for help from the law while they are close by?" she asked, figuring she already knew the answer but it didn't hurt to ask.

"We have no idea who R.S. is and what this person's connections might be," he said. Exactly the points she thought he'd make. "I have blood all over me and news of the murder will be out soon if it isn't already. If we so much as show our faces anywhere near a town around here, it'll cause a stir. I don't know about you, but the last thing I want is to spend hours on end in a sheriff's office explaining what the hell we were doing out here and why we ran away from a crime scene."

"I'm guessing there's no way they'll think he died from

the crash," she said realizing her mistake as the words left her mouth.

At the same time, they said, "Bullet."

"As soon as I can find bars, I'll be able to call for an extraction," he explained. "But this isn't like the military with units on the ready, so I don't want you to get your hopes up that someone will magically appear the minute I send out the signal if and when I get cell coverage again."

"I stopped believing in magic a long time ago, Vaughn." Those words came out with more emotion than she'd intended. That always happened when she thought about her parents for too long. It ruined her mood for the rest of the day and could last for days if she really let herself dwell.

Then again, it would be difficult to make this day get any worse. Her main comfort came from being with someone who knew what he was doing. Vaughn specialized in this line of work.

"Can I ask a question?" she said as he settled against a tree. He sat on the downed trunk with his legs outstretched and crossed at the ankles.

"Shoot," he said as he leaned his head back and closed his eyes.

"Why the military?" she asked. "As far as I remember, you couldn't stand being told what to do. Didn't you sign up to be told what to do every minute of the day for the rest of your life?"

"Easy. I had to get as far away from Lone Star Pass as possible," he said. "Means to an end."

Or did he mean get as far away from *her* as possible?

"I'll keep watch while you sleep," she said, redirecting the conversation.

"Keeping watch is just that...*watch*," he seemed to feel the need to point out. "If anything happens or there's any movement in the trees whatsoever, wake me immediately. Can you handle that?"

Oh, those last words were fingernails on a chalkboard.

"I'll do my best to obey your orders," she quipped.

"I didn't mean it like...oh hell, just wake me up, okay?"

"Fine," she said. The word every woman said when the opposite was true.

5

Vaughn blinked his eyes open. His eyelids were the equivalent of sandpaper. Gaining his bearings took all of two seconds. His gaze immediately searched for Katy. The way he'd snapped at her before dozing off made him wonder if she would ditch him once he fell asleep. He would only half blame her if she did after the way he'd come across. Being dropped into a situation before he had a chance to cool off from active duty wasn't good. He would normally be shipped off to a ranch for a week or so until he could lower his stress levels to the point he didn't snap someone in two for cutting him off in the grocery store line.

"Hey," he started as she pointed to a spot on his chest with a calm expression. "What?"

"You should see for yourself," she said like she was reading the ingredients off a cereal box.

He looked down to find a spider almost the size of his hand crawling up his stomach. No one got up from a tree trunk so fast. He flew to his feet and practically danced around until the thing was off him. When he looked over at her, she had a smirk on her face. "What the hell, Katy?"

"Um, you told me that I'm not supposed to *do* anything," she pointed out. "Remember that whole speech before you dozed off? The one where you explicitly told me to keep watch? Under no circumstances was I to act?"

"Smarty pants," he said after he took in a breath to calm his racing heart. "Are you happy with yourself right now?"

"I'm feeling pretty good actually, sitting up here on my high horse," she teased.

He couldn't help but chuckle, knowing full well he could be one intense sonofabitch. Her attempt to lighten the mood worked and he let the smile stick around.

"It wasn't venomous," she said. "I made sure of the fact before I let it crawl up your leg."

He dramatically shivered. She knew just how much he hated spiders.

"I'm glad you can be trusted for something," he said, hearing those words as they rolled off his tongue. She took them hard because she folded her arms over her chest again, as though creating a physical barrier to her heart. He could have explained that he didn't mean it to come out like that, but there was some truth to it. They both recognized it, so backtracking would only draw more attention to it.

"Looks like you're still afraid of spiders," she said. "I guess some things never change."

A snappy comeback came to mind but he stifled the urge. The joking mood had turned serious, and he wouldn't come across right. Instead of making matters worse between them, he decided to give it a rest. Plus, she was right. He still hated spiders. Although, where he'd just come from had plenty to spare.

"I'm awake now," he said, fishing his cell out of his

pocket and checking the time. "Looks like I slept for an hour."

"I wouldn't know," she said. "My cell is too close to being out of battery for me to keep it on. Once you find bars, I'll turn the power back on. Until then, I have to preserve what I can."

"I'm at sixty percent," he said, which wasn't a whole lot for the task ahead. They might not need half as much but he couldn't be sure. They wouldn't know if they had service until they walked into it, meaning he would have to keep his phone on and check regularly.

Both of them running out of battery would suck big time. Backup plans were for people who didn't trust they could switch gears, so he didn't waste time creating one. He did, however, need to assess the current situation.

"How hungry are you?" he asked, fishing his Swiss army knife out of his pocket.

"Starved, but I'll survive," she said. "How long do you think it'll be before we can be picked up?" She put her hand up to stop him from answering. "Right. There's no magic extraction team. We might have to be here for a while." She issued a sharp sigh, the kind that told him she was overwhelmed. It had been a day. She'd witnessed someone being shot and killed. They'd been—and possibly still were being—hunted. They'd been shot at and had driven over the side of a mountain. Now, he felt like an even bigger jerk for snapping at her.

Vaughn clenched his back teeth, promising to do better.

"Are you game for trying something?" he asked.

"I'd have to hear what it is," she said. He was noticing now how little she trusted him, even how little she'd trusted him back in the day, despite all their history. He'd been too young to realize what was happening back then. He'd been blind to the signs, the small references. He'd been so lost in his own intense feelings that he hadn't seen the little ways in which she shut down on him.

"Before I start a mission when I'm overseas, I always imagine what I'll be doing when it's done. It can be something as little as a movie I've been wanting to watch. I sort of make a date with my future self. I envision sitting in a recliner, eating popcorn. I know the exact brand of beer I'll be drinking. I can feel the cool bottle in my hand, the condensation as it rolls down the side. Details are important." He caught her gaze and saw a flash of vulnerability in her eyes. "Are you up for giving it a shot?"

"Can't hurt," she said on a shrug.

"Think about where you want to be tomorrow night," he said.

"My own bed, curled underneath the sheets," she said without hesitation.

"What are you wearing?" he asked, then put a hand up as he heard how that sounded. "It's part of the game. You have to be specific. I'm not hitting on you."

An emotion flashed behind her blues that he didn't want to spend too much time thinking about, since it looked a lot like disappointment.

"Okay," she said after a short pause. "I'm in my favorite cotton t-shirt and underwear, and nothing else. I like the feel of sheets against freshly shaved legs."

It was quite an image. One that wouldn't be so easy to erase now that it was stamped in his thoughts. He flexed and released his fingers a couple of times to work off some of the sudden tension.

"I'm fresh from a shower, and my hair is getting the pillowcase wet, but I don't care," she continued. "The room is cold and I pull the comforter all the way up to my neck. I love sleeping in a cold room underneath a pile of covers."

"I remember," he said as he realized he was getting a little too caught up in the moment. The image of stopping by early on a Saturday morning to sneak inside her room and be the first to wake her assaulted him.

"Not much has changed there," she said. He wondered if anything had. She was older now. She'd always been smart but he wondered if life had made her any wiser. "I guess some things never do change and you can probably fall asleep sitting up. In fact, I just watched you and I'm still amazed at how an hour of sleep can revive you."

"You do what you have to," he said. "Calving season taught me all I needed to know about going without sleep. I know exactly the point at which I need to rest. The military taught me how far my body could go injured before I needed to power down."

Her smile was like the sun breaking through the clouds in spring. "Calving season." Her smile widened. "Those were good times."

"Sure, for someone who liked to prank me," he said. "I was easy pickings."

"You know you liked it," she quipped.

Now that the mood was lighter again, he cut a section of bark off a tree and ran his blade across the inside of the piece. "This might hold you over until we can get real food."

"I'll try anything," she said, taking the offering he held out. "But we should get going. The faster we get out of here, the quicker we can find coverage and *really* get out of this place.

In theory, that was the idea. The truth was they could end up lost and stranded. Or, worse yet, end up as bear food.

KATY FOLLOWED Vaughn as they tracked further west. He stopped every once in a while to check for cell coverage. Every chirp or broken twig sent her blood pressure through the roof. They'd been walking for a solid hour before he took anything that resembled a real break.

"We haven't seen anything resembling a town since we started," she pointed out.

"True," he conceded. "But we don't need an actual town to find bars."

"I know," she said. "It's just that I'm starting to have visions of a big fat hamburger. The kind where the juice runs down your arm when you try to eat it if you're not careful. My mouth is watering and I don't even eat meat anymore."

"When did that happen?" he asked, sounding caught off guard.

"After I left Lone Star Pass," she admitted. There was no way in hell she was going to tell him the real reason for her vegetarianism was that every time she thought about hamburgers or beef, her mind snapped back to the cattle ranch and the fact she missed him beyond words.

"You just stopped liking it?" he asked as his brow quirked.

"Something like that," she said. It was as far as she was willing to go. "Doesn't matter."

He mumbled something she couldn't quite make out and, based on his tone, probably didn't want to.

"People change," she said by way of defense.

"I guess so," he replied with a shrug.

Katy let the subject drop. "I wish I had water. My throat is so dry, it's like Texas soil in August during a heatwave."

"Every summer in Texas is a heatwave," he joked but it fell flat. She wasn't in the mood to laugh any longer. Not when Vaughn was flip-flopping, trying to decide if he could stand being around her. To be fair, she'd been the one to leave him, and she'd intentionally cut him to the quick with her words, saying she never loved him in the first place. The devastation on his eighteen-year-old face had almost caused her to take her words back. Leaving town, walking away from Vaughn, was the hardest thing she'd ever done. Cutting off all communication with the one person who had been her person might have been for the best, but the void it left was a cavern that had never refilled.

The fear of turning into her parents had stifled her. A therapist had told her that she would never be able to allow love into her life until she forgave them.

Maybe some people were meant to be alone. She'd dated over the years. Spent time with people. After a few months, it was always time to move on. Leave before things could get ugly and the fights started. Leave before she could commit too many feelings to someone. To be fair, she never dated anyone who might pull real emotions out of her.

"I said we should get going."

Vaughn's voice cut through her heavy thoughts as he snapped his fingers as though to awaken her from a trance.

"Sorry," she said, pushing up to standing. The realization she'd kept everyone at arm's length struck hard. On some level, she must have known that was exactly what she'd been doing. On another level, she didn't want to admit the therapist might have been right. But the bigger shock to her system was that despite Vaughn's prickly exterior when it came to interactions with her, she'd never felt this comfortable with anyone since him. It was just shared history and probably nothing else. She'd cut herself off from everyone back home. Her uncle was the only one she ever stayed in contact with after her parents' deaths.

"No need to apologize," he said. "You're tired and hungry. You've been through hell recently, especially today. The past twelve hours would send anyone into shock. Here you are, hanging in there like nobody's business. You're doing better than you think right now."

Those words reassured her, bringing comfort like she hadn't felt in ages. Maybe ever. Even with Vaughn, she'd held back all those years ago. Still, he'd been the closest to breaking down her walls. And look how she'd treated him.

"It has been a long day," she finally admitted. She pulled out her cell and turned it on. She checked the screen absently, not expecting much. "Hold on. I have half a bar."

Vaughn immediately rechecked his cell.

"I've got nothing over here," he said, moving beside her. He was all spice and warmth as he stood next to her. "Look at that." He held up his cell and took two steps back. "I have a whole bar here. Should be enough to make the call."

Katy reminded herself there wouldn't be an instant pickup. This was good news, though. Very good news.

Surprisingly, she wasn't as afraid out here as she probably would have been. Vaughn made the difference. Could she trust him a little? Would it even matter? He wasn't the type to forgive and forget. He was far too proud for that, which sucked for her, because she sure could use a friend right now. Then again, based on the past and how deeply she hurt him, she didn't deserve his forgiveness. The breakup had come out of the blue for him, while she'd been contemplating it for weeks.

Vaughn spoke quietly into the phone, stepping away from her. She strained to listen but couldn't make out what he was saying. It wouldn't shock her if he was ready to be done. Was he making separate arrangements for them? Was he ready to ship her off? She couldn't blame him if he was and yet she knew deep down he would never do that to her. It wasn't in his makeup to leave someone stranded, even if it was her.

The only reason—and she couldn't stress that enough—he was here in the first place was a personal call for help by her uncle. Speaking of whom, could she call him? She checked her cell for any text messages. Her old cell was long gone. It had been the first thing Vaughn had thrown out when he first showed up at her apartment. Not 'thrown out' exactly. He'd strapped it to the underside of a trash collector truck. So, it made the rounds and anyone trying to find her would have to follow the trashmen.

At the time, she didn't realize how serious this whole ordeal was. Her uncle had called and explained that she needed to go with Vaughn. It had been so long since she'd heard that name, it took a few seconds for it to sink in. She went through several stages; disbelief, then denial before acceptance. The last twinge of denial came when he stood at her backdoor, knocking, and there was no denying he was right there.

Vaughn ended his call and then turned toward her. "Good news. There's a guy here in Colorado who can get to us in the next hour. All we have to do is walk up to that peak and then wait for him."

"An hour?" she asked. "That's nothing."

"As long as no one gets to us before he does, we'll be fine."

Katy had started to feel like they wouldn't die on the side of a mountain until Vaughn said those words. Now? Not so much.

Vaughn tucked his cell phone in his pocket and urged

her to do the same. Next, he caught her off guard when he reached for her hand and then linked their fingers. Her hand was small by comparison. And yet it fit into his perfectly. His was strong and calloused, and skilled as she remembered. Goose bumps ran up her arm at thinking back to how incredible his touch had been. Trying to shove those thoughts aside, she refocused on the patch of mountain in front of her.

Going up was hard on Vaughn's thigh, so they took their time with frequent stops. It took forty-five minutes to reach the peak. As they got close, Vaughn squeezed her hand. She knew he was telling her not to say a word.

She could hear her own breathing along with her heartbeat as it thundered.

A man stood half behind a tree. It was impossible to get a good look at him. This must be their contact. So, why was Vaughn being so cautious?

6

Vaughn couldn't get a good look at his contact from this vantage point and something seemed off. His training had taught him to take nothing for granted. Before checking out the guy, he placed the flat of Katy's palm on the tree in front of them. He placed his hand over hers for a few seconds to let her know to stay put. Electricity pinged up his arm from contact, but he ignored it.

She gave a slight nod but he could almost feel her beginning to tremble. It nearly gutted him that she had to go through this.

Crouching down, his thigh burned as he army crawled in a circle until he was behind the pickup man. At least, he hoped this was the contact. Their communication should be secure on his cell. Katy hadn't made the phone call to her uncle yet. Plus, he'd given her a new phone with two numbers programmed inside, his and the one belonging to her relative.

Coming up from behind, he realized what was bugging him about the man. He wasn't moving. As in, at all. His chest wasn't moving up and down as it would if he was breathing. Vaughn bit back a curse, fearing the worst.

And then he heard a noise to his right. He hoped like hell that Katy had stayed put and hadn't decided to follow him. She could end up risking both of their lives.

Vaughn drew his Sig and pointed the barrel in the direction of the sound. He caught sight of a glint of metal, and realized a gun was being aimed right back at him. Had the contact put out a dummy to throw off the others in case they found him first?

He reached for his cell as it vibrated. There was a text: *That you, Alpha Dog?*

Sighing relief, he lowered his weapon and sent confirmation. A few seconds after receiving it, his contact stepped out of the darkness. Vaughn moved stealthily along the tree line until he reached the former Jarhead, who went by the nickname Psycho. Good name to have on Vaughn's side.

They shook hands in silence before he held up a finger to indicate he'd be right back. Another trip around and back, and he brought Katy over. She seemed to realize talking was a bad idea. Being near the peak left them exposed. They couldn't stay long.

Psycho motioned for them to follow, so they did. They walked longer than Vaughn wanted to but there was a truck stashed off the road. Psycho took the driver's seat, while he and Katy slipped underneath the tarp in the back onto a foam mattress complete with covers. It wasn't her bed and there were no sheets, but it was the closest she could come under the circumstances to giving her some sense of normalcy.

Once they were safely tucked inside, she surprised him by scooting over to his side. It was probably just for warmth, so he helped her lift up enough to put his arm around her.

She settled into the crook of his arm, causing his heart to race just like old times.

"Try to get some sleep, okay," he said quietly into her ear.

She responded by nodding. Her body relaxed into his and some of the tension in her muscles eased. It felt good to have her in his arms again. Too good. But he wouldn't disturb her because her steady even breathing said she was already asleep. It was his turn to keep watch over her while she got a few hours of shuteye.

Vaughn had no idea where they were being taken. Most likely to a safehouse so suitable arrangements could be made. Would they stay inside Colorado? Most likely, the answer was yes. Law enforcement would assume the killer had fled, so it would be easy to hide under everyone's noses. Especially if they didn't have to leave a house for a few days. He needed medical attention on his thigh. It was nothing he couldn't handle on his own with the right supplies. His stitches burst open, and that was the reason for all the blood earlier. The t-shirt was keeping enough pressure on the wound to stem the bleeding. Normally, he'd go higher up on the thigh, but this wasn't a fresh injury. It was a few days old. Once again, he thought about how pretty much everything on this mission had gone FUBAR.

They were alive. That was saying something. There were trained assassins hired to take them out. Now, he was up to speed on the stakes. He wasn't sure what her uncle had gotten into but it wasn't good and it was definitely with the wrong people. Politicians had to keep a whole lot of people happy. They used folks who they sometimes burned in the end. Ask a certain democratic president from the sixties who'd been assassinated, how it worked out when someone played both sides and lost.

Vaughn wasn't sure how long they'd been in the back of the pickup before it stopped, but his best guess would be a couple of hours. He needed a shower, medical supplies, and fresh clothes. Food and coffee would be bonuses, and he assumed Katy needed the latter far more than he did.

When the truck stopped, she was mildly snoring, which was a sign of just how exhausted she was. Once he got the green light from Psycho, Vaughn opened the tarp. They were in a garage that led to an apartment, which was separated from the main house.

"You'll be fine in here," Psycho said. "It'll buy a bit of time. My wife knows better than to come inside or poke her nose around. There's a mini-apartment up there with food and all the supplies you need. If there's something I can get for you, I'd appreciate if you'd text rather than come out looking. I got kids."

It was hard to imagine a man as gruff as Psycho as a father, but, hey, Vaughn had no right to judge anyone else's life choices. He didn't see himself as father material, but that was his choice. Psycho could do whatever he wanted.

Strange, though, because there was a time when he thought he had his whole life mapped out. He'd planned to ask Katy to marry him once she got out of college, which had been important to her all those years ago. He wouldn't exactly call her predictable, but he'd believed they had something special and that there was a time when she would have said yes. Looking back now, he could see that she'd evaded his questions skillfully when it came to ever having a family or being together for the long haul.

He lifted her out of the truck with ease, despite her being dead weight. Of course, his thigh wouldn't exactly agree. It was angry and looking for any excuse to complain.

Psycho nodded toward a flight of stairs that would, no doubt, lead to an apartment.

"Okay to turn the lights on or are we incognito all the way?" Vaughn asked.

"Lights are good," he said. "My family knows to avoid this whole area, especially if there are lights on. You might want to keep the shades pulled and the lights dim at night."

"Got it," Vaughn said.

"Stay as long as you think you need to but not a second more. I've had a bad feeling lately and it's probably nothing but you know how superstitious we get sometimes," Psycho said, his tattooed arm sleeves were vines with roses peeking out every once in a while. Despite the frigid temperatures, he wore a modified sweatshirt that had the arms cut out, as well as the collar. At approximately forty-five years old, he had a small potbelly with overly muscular biceps that looked something out of a cartoon. "All I ask is that you protect my family as though it was your own."

"You know it," Vaughn agreed. Giving his word meant everything. He also realized those gut feelings were often correct and kept them alive.

Psycho nodded. His look of gratitude meant the world to Vaughn, an unspoken mutual respect and understanding that sealed them together.

Vaughn carried Katy up the stairs that led into an open-concept space. Psycho walked over to a lamp and turned it on rather than flip on an overhead, which Vaughn appreciated. The softer light shouldn't disturb Katy. She needed rest as much as flowers needed sunlight.

A quick scan revealed a clean and well-organized space. There was a bed to his right tucked away in a corner that was made up and ready to go. He walked over to it and gently set Katy down. She immediately curled up on her side and he resisted the urge to linger. She seemed so peaceful in that moment. Pride filled his chest that he was able to give her a warm bed for the night. He slipped her shoes off and tucked her underneath the covers. It wasn't a shower and fresh clothes, but this was the best he could do under the circumstances.

Then, he joined Psycho in the kitchenette.

"There's every necessity here," Psycho said, opening the fridge. "My beautiful wife stocked a few meals for you. She always keeps extras in case." *In case* happened more often than not to men with careers like theirs. This place was clearly used as a safehouse. Vaughn would ask no questions about any past residents, why this existed in the first place, or who funded it. His need-to-know-basis military training kicked in.

He was also struck by just how badass the men in his own unit were, and how these same men who killed on an almost daily basis at times to protect freedoms, were basically mush when they talked about their wives or girlfriends back home. As for Vaughn, he kept a no-attachment-necessary mentality. He was always clear upfront that there would be no strings. If someone wasn't cool with it, he moved on, no need to hurt someone. If, on the other hand, someone was up for great sex and occasional drop-ins when it suited both of them, he was game. He'd found that being honest from the get-go was always the best course of action. Once the other person had all the information, they could make an informed decision as to whether they wanted to play along. A couple of times, lines were crossed where he started to develop feelings beyond casual sex or he sensed that the other party did. A quick but permanent goodbye solved either issue.

Vaughn could admit to being lonely at times. With his

thirtieth birthday looming, he was beginning to want more than an adrenaline rush out of life. Settling down and marriage wasn't on his radar but he wondered if there was something in between.

"I appreciate this more than you know," he said, tuning back into the conversation with Psycho, who had detailed out where coffee and other essential supplies were located.

An oversized loveseat with a coffee table made up the living space. A small flatscreen hung on the wall. There was a desk pushed up against a wall with a large window that no doubt overlooked the backyard.

In Colorado, this would be called a carriage house. Texas would name it an apartment over the garage. Either way, he didn't take the space for granted.

"Are there exits other than the stairwell?" Vaughn had to ask. It was easier than figuring it out for himself, although he'd do his own assessment once Psycho was gone.

Psycho walked over to the desk. He shoved it aside and lifted a floor panel of the wood-looking vinyl. "This works like a slide, so be ready. A false panel in the back automatically opens if you push this here." He pointed to a piece of metal in the shape of a handle. "That way, there's less noise to alert..." He flashed his eyes. "I have Dobermans in the house. If this gets tripped, I let them out and they know what to do. Make sure you get over the back fence before they get to you. They won't know the difference between a good guy and a bad one. They'll go after the smell of fear, which I'm guessing won't be a problem for you, but might be for your friend over there."

Vaughn nodded. He'd gotten a little too good at controlling his emotions, stuffing them down so deep they would never see the light of day again. So, it struck him as odd that he had so much chemistry with Katy after all these years.

Some of those same emotions surfaced, and he didn't know what the hell to do with them.

All he knew for certain was finding a bed for her made him feel better than he'd felt in too many years to count.

"Will I end up barbecued if I touch any part of the fence?" he had to ask.

Psycho smiled. "I guess we all really do think alike." He nodded. "There's enough of a delay that you should be fine if you head straight there and hop right over. But, yeah, you might want to avoid direct contact."

"Got it."

"The good news is there's a dirt bike stashed in the woods about a hundred yards directly south," Psycho said. "Keys are tucked underneath the front wheel. There's a helmet on the back. Only one, though."

"Let's hope I don't need to know this, let alone use it," Vaughn said. "I need a day to regroup and then I suspect we'll be out of your hair."

Psycho closed up the hole in the floor, stood up, and then replaced the desk.

"No skin off my nose if you need longer," he said.

"Much appreciated," Vaughn replied with a handshake.

"Medical kit is underneath the sink in the bathroom," Psycho said before heading toward the door. "It's more advanced than most and should have everything you need to take care of that." He motioned toward Vaughn's thigh. "Fresh clothes in there, too. For both of you. Not sure about sizes or fit, but the clothes are clean and there's no blood on them."

"They'll do fine," he confirmed.

"Text if you need anything," Psycho said before the two shook hands one last time. He was being cordial. They both knew Vaughn wouldn't ask for anything else. Not with all this that was already being offered.

They had maybe twenty-four hours if they were lucky to clean up, rest up, and come up with a plan to find out who R.S. was. Katy's uncle might have the answers. Vaughn checked the news to see what was being released about the murder. Hells bells.

Things just got a whole lot worse.

∽

KATY SMELLED what she was pretty certain was heaven. Eggs. Coffee. And something else she couldn't quite put her finger on. She opened her eyes and panicked. For a split-second, she'd lost all sense of where she was and what had happened. The only grace about being a heavy sleeper was that she rarely remembered her dreams.

She sat up and witnessed Vaughn's muscled back, shirtless, standing in front of the stove. He had on a fresh pair of painter's paints that were a size too big at the waist and a hair too short, and yet they somehow still worked on his solid-built frame.

The shades were drawn. The clock read six o'clock on the dot. In the soft light, she could barely force her gaze away from the ripples of muscle. Her chest squeezed at the image because for a split second her mind wished this was the norm.

Realization dawned that they were in someone's apartment. This must be where the contact from last night took them. A shower and a toothbrush would have to wait. She searched for her cell phone, found it on the small night table next to her bed along with a charger that was plugged in. Now, she really had gone to heaven.

As soon as she moved, Vaughn turned around. He turned off the burner and moved the pan before locking gazes with her. The solemn look on his face struck with force.

"It won't do any good to call your uncle," he said. "He's missing."

Katy blinked a couple of times like that would somehow help with hearing the news. "I'm sorry, what?"

"When he didn't show up for work, his administrative assistant sent someone to check on him. His home was broken into and there were signs of a struggle," he informed with compassion in his voice—compassion that threatened to tear down a few more of the carefully constructed walls she'd so carefully built around her heart.

She checked her phone in case there was a text or phone call from him. "He didn't try to reach out."

"He was aware of the plan to get you to safety in case this whole ordeal wasn't over," Vaughn said. "Looks like we made the right call."

"Except that my uncle might be dead by now," she said.

Vaughn shook his head. "I wouldn't be so certain. If they'd wanted to kill him, they would have done it in his home. A gun with a silencer would do the trick without waking the neighbors."

"Why would they do that?" she asked.

Before he could answer, the reason dawned on her.

"They're trying to force me out of hiding," she said. His quick nod and compressed lips told her she was right on track.

"I came to the same conclusion," he stated. "There are probably all kinds of thoughts and a whole lot of guilt racing around in that beautiful head of yours. No one works well on an empty stomach. Let's get food inside you and some caffeine. Then, we'll start brainstorming ideas."

So many thoughts fought for center stage. But he was right. Her stomach growled, reminding her just how empty it was. She wanted, no needed, strength so she could think with a clear head.

"Okay," she said, glancing around for the bathroom. She couldn't stand the thought of eating with these grimy teeth.

"Bathroom is right behind that door. Supplies are in the medicine cabinet. Your toothbrush is still in the wrapper," he said.

Katy pushed up to standing and sat right back down. Lack of food and water was taking its toll. Vaughn was by her side before she could look up. He handed her a bottle of water after taking the lid off.

"You're most likely dehydrated," he said. "This should help."

She downed the entire bottle in two seconds flat. The next time she stood up, he held her steady by the arm and walked her to the door.

"Okay?" he asked.

"I got this," she said after thanking him.

A splash of cold water and clean teeth worked wonders for her mood. She saw clean clothes folded up on a basket to one side of the small but efficient bathroom. If she extended her arms in the center of the room, she could almost touch walls on all sides. Food. Caffeine. A shower.

The eggs, hash browns, and ham slices were almost too good to be true. This wasn't the time to worry about eating meat with her vegetarian diet. She needed the protein. Her food plan only worked when she could eat every few hours. Since they would be leaving here at some point, she figured she needed all the strength she could get. Who knew when they'd have a sit-down meal like this again?

The coffee was even better.

"Mind if I grab a shower?" she asked, figuring she could take the cup with her. She glanced over by the desk and saw a backpack that she assumed was filled with supplies. Their shoes sat next to it along with coats. An emergency escape pack? The answer was most likely yes and it was a stark reminder of their currently predicament. "I'll feel better once I'm clean and in fresh clothes. I assume the ones in the bathroom are for me."

He nodded as an emotion flickered behind his eyes that looked a lot like need. The same feeling circled low in her belly and warmed her thighs at the thought of being alone in a safe place with Vaughn.

"Go ahead," he said. "Towels are in the cabinet above the commode."

She stood up and managed to walk across the room without getting woozy this time, a definite improvement from a few minutes ago.

As she undressed, she kicked the bathroom door closed with her big toe. After a few sips of coffee, she was already starting to feel half human again. He was right about the food and the caffeine. With her uncle in trouble, there was no way she could clear her mind completely. Waking it up was a good start.

During the shower, her thoughts kept coming back to R.S. The best way to find out who this person was would be to go to her uncle's home and check out his computer. Or maybe figure out a way to hack into the contacts in his cell. Showing up in Austin might be exactly what the bastards expected, so she shelved the idea. Unless, of course, she could hide her identity.

No. It seemed impossible.

What else could they do? She rounded back to the idea of having someone hack into his calendar and his contacts. Of course, someone who targeted a politician and had ex-military on the payroll would know how to hide their tracks.

She needed to think outside the box on this one. What about her uncle's financials? Campaign contributions? His campaign manager should have access to all the money records. Maybe that was the angle she could go with to locate R.S.

At least this gave some direction. She wouldn't exactly say it provided hope, but Vaughn would most likely have ideas of his own on how to trace R.S. In fact, he most likely already had someone working on it.

This person had to be prominent, have money, and be able to hide behind others.

7

By the time Katy returned to the kitchen, Vaughn had washed and put away the dishes. He glanced at the empty coffee cup in her hand, forcing his gaze away from the way those black leggings fit like a second skin. "Refill?"

"Please," she said, then chewed on the inside of her cheek. He didn't need her 'tell' to realize her brain would be humming at this point.

He poured a second cup and motioned toward the round table with two chairs where they'd eaten breakfast. She joined him and he set the mugs down.

"You have a lot going on up there," he said, pointing to her forehead. "But it's always best to take a step back when emotions take the wheel."

She clamped her lips shut as she lifted up her cup, rolling it between her palms like she needed the warmth.

"Emotions are the enemy to logical planning," he reiterated.

"Got it," she said. "Emotions are bad."

"In this case...yes," he said. "When emotions are heightened, mistakes are made. It's the reason we learn to compartmentalize ours in the service."

She nodded.

"Thank you, by the way," she said. "For your service. I'm not sure I've had a chance to tell you just how proud I am of you for serving the country, when you could have stepped into a cushy future on the ranch."

"I don't know if you've kept up with anything about the Firebrand family, but I wouldn't exactly call what we have an easy life," he said with a little more anger than intended. It wasn't directed at her. When it came to his family life, he was angry at the world. "Have you heard about what's been going on?"

"There was no reason to keep up with anyone, but some news has been unavoidable," she admitted.

"Like the fact my mother is in jail for attempted murder," he said flat out.

"I'm so sorry. I remember the two of you weren't close, but that must feel awful. No matter what else, she is your mother," she said with a look of sympathy.

"Unfortunately, yes," he said. "By birth, at least." He paused for a few seconds before adding, "And thank you, by the way." Jackie Firebrand married his father for the name and the money. It certainly wasn't to bring up the nine sons she'd had. Considering she didn't seem to want to take care of one, he had no idea why she'd kept going except to try to match or outdo his Aunt Lucia. She was everything his mother wasn't...doting, present. His aunt was one of the most down-to-earth people anyone could ever meet. He and his Uncle Brodie hadn't always seen eye-to-eye, but welcome to the Firebrand men. His relationship with his father was almost to the point of irreparable.

"Again, I'm sorry, Vaughn," she said, reaching across the

table and touching his hand. He pulled back. Skin-to-skin contact with Katy was a bad idea. His body didn't seem to remember how she'd stomped all over his heart all those years ago because it reacted to her in ways he hadn't experienced in years.

"Not your fault," he said.

"Still," she responded with the soft, sleepy voice that always shot an arrow straight through his heart. "It's hard when your parents aren't what you would like them to be."

That was the understatement of the year.

"Trust me. I have a lot of experience there," she added.

"What about yours?" he asked, turning the tables. He'd said all he wanted to about his own mother.

"Gone," she said, her eyebrows drawing together. "I thought you knew."

"No. I didn't keep up with anyone once I left town," he admitted. "Hell, not even my own siblings and cousins."

"It's probably for the best, you know?" she asked but it was more statement than question.

"Why?" he asked, curious. She never really talked about her family much back in high school. She was an only child. Her parents didn't have an idyllic marriage.

"They were awful together," she said without hesitation. "Gasoline and match."

Katy rolled up the long-sleeve cotton shirt to expose an inch-long scar above her left elbow. "Remember this?"

"Yes. You said you fell on the playground in elementary school and landed on one of those metal bolts," he said.

"I wasn't exactly being honest," she said. "The truth is that my father gave me this by throwing me across the room. I landed on the sharp side of a fireplace poker. The two of them had been in a doozy of a fight. I got a C on a social studies test in middle school. My father had been drinking.

He shouted at me as he worked himself up on how ungrateful I was for everything he did for me."

Vaughn's hands fisted. "I don't remember him breaking his neck to help you with anything."

"Because he didn't," she stated.

"Where was your mother during all this?" he asked through gritted teeth. His second question had to do with asking why he was finding this out now.

"Striking him in the back with anything she could find," she admitted, dropping her gaze to the table where she'd twisted her fingers. This wasn't easy for her. Her body language made him want to scoot his chair around the table and hold her.

Her chin quivered and his heart nearly broke in half. Anger flooded him at what she'd had to endure because he sensed this was only the tip of the iceberg.

"What about those marks on your lower back?" he asked as rage became a rising tide inside him. "The ones you said were from falling into a barbed wire fence in ninth grade?"

She looked at him with eyes that were a mix of apology, pain, and embarrassment. It suddenly occurred to him why she would hide this. She was embarrassed and maybe ashamed to talk about it all those years ago. Most high schoolers would hide this rather than risk being yanked from the only life they'd ever known by social services.

"No child should ever be put through physical abuse," he managed to get out through gritted teeth. "Least of all you."

Katy picked up her cup of coffee and studied the rim for a few seconds before taking a sip. Her face twisted. "It's cold." All the warmth drained from her expression until she recovered a more serious look. "I can get another..."

"Don't get up," he instructed as he grabbed her mug

from the table after she set it down. "You walked a long time yesterday. You should preserve your strength."

"Me?" she asked with a frown. Her gaze dropped down to his thigh where the bullet had pierced. "What about you?"

"The supplies here are good," he said. "I'm all fixed up."

Being here in this apartment together felt a lot like it might if they moved in together. The random thought caught him off guard. And yet he couldn't deny being around Katy again felt right in more ways than one. It was easy to slip into old patterns with her.

Dangerous too.

Rather than let his guard down, he refilled her mug and brought it over to the table before reclaiming his seat. "As far as your parents go, I want to be sad they're gone but if they inflicted those wounds on you…" He had to take a deep breath before continuing as he felt his blood pressure rise. "Let's just say that I'd rather be alone in a room with your father for ten minutes than let him so much as look at you again."

"I appreciate the sentiment, Vaughn," she started. "I really do." She shrugged. "It's fine, though."

"No. It's not," he said as he moved next to her and took a knee.

"He called me a bastard child behind my back," she said. "It got me wondering if my mother had had an affair. Maybe the father I knew wasn't my biological parent."

"It's possible," he said before lifting her arm and running a finger along the scar above her elbow. Rather than overthink his next move, he brought his lips down on the raised skin. He had no idea how a father could harm his own child, let alone a daughter. A dark family secret like paternity might explain it, even though it wasn't an excuse.

There was no reason good enough to bring harm to a child. "This makes you even more beautiful in my opinion."

A red blush crawled up her neck.

"I'm sorry that I failed you," he said. "I should have known what was going on when you were making up excuses." A whole lot of their history started clicking into place. All those times she suddenly had to ditch their dates, making up a lame excuse about homework or her parents freaking out over a grade and grounding her for the night. She'd been protecting him from the truth—a truth that would have gotten him in a whole mess of trouble back then. Hormones and teenage boys led to tempers that flared. Vaughn wasn't a jerk to anyone who didn't deserve it. But, damn, he wished he'd known about this sooner.

"You didn't," she said, bringing her free hand to lift his chin up so they were looking into each other's eyes. It was as though a bomb detonated in his chest.

∾

KATY COULDN'T LET Vaughn take the fall for something he didn't do. "You had no idea what was going on. I pretty much saw to it that no one knew."

"I should have realized," he countered, clearly not ready to let himself off the hook just yet.

"How could you?" she asked. "I became an expert at lying to cover. No one knew."

"Sure, but I was the closest one to you," he said. "At one time the two of us were almost inseparable."

"You trusted me," she said, realizing how much it hurt to say those words. It was very clear to her that ship had sailed after the breakup. He was only being nice now because he felt sorry for her, which she hated. "I used that to keep you in the dark." She stood up and walked away from him. Admitting to him that she'd lied to the one person she loved wasn't something she could do while staring into those eyes. In fact, she needed to put as much distance between them as she could so she could breathe. The air was thinning at the table, and it was becoming difficult to take in air.

She ducked her head to cover the fact a rogue tear was making its way down her cheek. The last thing she wanted was for him to see her crying. Her mother's tears after Katy had been beaten or berated were emotional blackmail.

Katy never let anyone see her cry.

Before she could tell him to stay back, Vaughn was beside her.

"I did," he said with a hint of melancholy in his tone. She realized he would never make that mistake again. He would never blindly give his trust after she'd betrayed it. "And the past is in the past, where it belongs, except when it affects the present."

Exactly what she was thinking. Exactly the reason he wouldn't go there with her ever again.

"What your parents did," he began, "and I'm guessing this is the tip of the iceberg when it comes to the hell you went through—"

She nodded.

"—their mark will leave a lasting imprint," he continued.

What could she do about it now? "They're gone. There's no way to go back and change what happened or how I responded to their actions."

"What would you do differently if you could?" he asked. She realized the answer he was searching for was that she would be honest with him. There was no way she could admit that to him right now. Not when there was a hint of hope in his voice.

"There's no point, Vaughn," she said, turning to walk away. "We aren't time travelers."

He caught her by the arm. She stopped in her tracks, frozen. It must have dawned on him why this would be her instinctive reaction because he let go.

"I wasn't trying to hurt you," he said quietly.

"I know," she said. "At least, I figured it out. Sometimes it takes my brain a minute to catch up." She turned to face him as another rogue tear released, falling down her cheek. He thumbed it away.

The fatal mistake was locking eyes this close as he rested the side of his hand on her shoulder.

"Hey," he started. "We might not be able to go back and change the past, but we can apologize for being clueless. Trust or not, I should have seen what was going on with you. I could have been a better boyfriend."

Sensual shivers skittered across her skin as she stood there, so close they were breathing the same air.

"Vaughn," she said as she heard the frog in her throat. "This is probably the worst of ideas, but I'd like it very much if you would kiss me right now."

He leaned forward until his forehead rested against hers. "I would very much like the same thing. Which is exactly the reason we can't."

How was that for a confusing answer? "I'm not sure I follow."

"You're vulnerable right now and searching for something familiar, for comfort," he said. "I just can't be that for you."

"Oh," she said, realizing she might have crossed a boundary unintentionally. "I didn't see a ring, so I assumed you were single."

"I am," he confirmed.

Embarrassment flamed, sending warmth to her cheeks.

"Then, you just don't want to," she said, taking a step back. "I shouldn't have asked, Vaughn. That was out of line." She took another step back. "I shouldn't have asked a question like that."

"Consent is sexy," he said, and his voice was gruff. It reminded her exactly of what he used to sound like while they spent time actually kissing when they were young... deep and gravelly. "We have too much history to take something like that lightly." Those words made her feel a little better. If that was his goal, he was succeeding. "Besides, when I do kiss you, it won't be out of a need to ground ourselves. It'll be because I can't stop myself from tasting those cherry lips of yours again."

In the willpower department, he was definitely winning.

But he was probably helping them both avoid a big mistake. It was a little too easy to slip into old routines when he was near. It was a little too easy to wish he would wrap those strong arms around her until she finally felt safe again —a feeling she'd only had in his arms. It was a little too easy to get lost in Vaughn Firebrand.

At least one of them had their senses.

"Don't worry," she started as she walked over to the table and picked up her coffee cup, rolling it around in her palms. "You're safe with me. I won't try that again."

"Shame," he said, so low she almost didn't hear.

Was that an invitation to test his willpower later?

8

Vaughn cleared his throat, and then rejoined Katy at the kitchen table. The kiss had been a temptation he couldn't afford. Not after she'd opened up to him, exposing a vulnerability that had been next to impossible to resist. He'd had to pull on every ounce of willpower left in him to avoid making a mistake—and kissing her would be a mistake. Since he wasn't a glutton for punishment and his resolve was dwindling by the second, he forced his gaze from those full pink lips of hers. Besides, she was reacting to the loss of life she'd seen yesterday and the stress of her uncle's disappearance.

In no way, shape, or form did she actually want to be with Vaughn. She was searching for what was known as proof of life. He'd heard about it. Read about it. Experienced it. So, he knew the trap a little too well.

Besides, when he kissed Katy, he needed to know it was because the two of them were in their right minds, and not as a stress reaction on her part. Vaughn stopped himself right there. He was getting a little too philosophical for his own good. He'd never been one to stop and overthink kissing a beautiful woman before. And Katy still caused his pulse to race when she was within arm's reach. His reaction to her was dangerous. Even more so now that he knew what she'd been dealing with all those years ago. Keeping himself in check and his focus on the mission outranked everything else.

Maybe when this was all said and done, they could talk about...

He stopped himself right there. Just because she'd shared a few secrets didn't mean everything would be hunky dory between them now or ever again. Accepting this mission was a favor to her uncle—an uncle who had always been decent to Vaughn when the man visited Lone Star Pass. None of this was about rekindling a relationship with Katy. Period. If he needed to remind himself of the fact every day, he would. Hell, if the reminder needed to come every hour, he would do that too.

As far as her uncle went, Vaughn had sensed that she was more comfortable around her mother's brother back then. So, naturally, Vaughn liked the man. Now that he knew the hell she was being put through at home, he understood more of why she would lean on her relative.

"Why did they take him?" she asked. "Is it to bring me out of hiding?"

"That's my best guess," he said, refocusing on the mission. "Dagger is working on hacking into your uncle's cell phone records as well as his home computer to see what kind of information he can dig up."

"I doubt he'll be able to break into the one from his work, since it's encrypted by the government," she said.

Vaughn cracked a smile. "You'd be surprised at the magic Dagger is able to work when he puts his mind to it."

She nodded but didn't look up at him.

"The issue is whether or not the folks on the other side who are causing all this chaos are better with computers than Dagger," he explained. It always came down to who had the best skills or training.

"How long do we have to stay here?" Katy asked, motioning toward the rucksack next to the desk. "How long is it safe?"

"You noticed that," he said. "Probably not a real long time. Psycho gave a warning this area might be hot. I have an escape plan in case we have to bolt out of here on a moment's notice, which might be all we get before a raid or the bastards from before catch up to us."

She looked up at him with a dullness to her features that made him realize the wall had come back up between them. Or was it her fear response? Did she basically force herself to go dead inside as a coping mechanism? She'd done the same years ago but sold it as being stressed about school. Little had he known she was dealing with so much more at home than pressure to make good grades.

Another round of guilt slammed into him for not noticing it. Chalking it up to being young was a convenient excuse, so he didn't go there. He wouldn't let himself off the hook so easily. Ever since he was old enough to grow hair on his chest, he took responsibility for his actions.

"Do you think they'll hurt him?" she asked, not needing to point out that she was referring to her uncle.

He couldn't answer with complete honesty without causing worry that might not be needed. The truth of the matter was that the bastards might hurt him. Killing him was a different story. He couldn't see what they would have to gain by doing that. The minute Katy surfaced might be a whole different story. "People like that usually hold onto their leverage for as long as necessary."

"Meaning they'll hurt him if I surface," she surmised. "Possibly even kill him."

He issued a sharp sigh, realizing he was between a rock and a hard place on this answer. "I don't know who we're dealing with, so I can't exactly say for certain one way or the other. I'm not trying to dodge answering your question, but at the same time I don't want to give an answer that will cause you to worry if it's unnecessary."

Katy compressed her lips and turned to look away. She was processing what he'd told her and that was a good thing.

"We could play the *what if* scenario all day long, but it will only exhaust our brains," he continued. "This might be a good time to shrink the world down to what we know, and not make too many assumptions beyond that information."

Quiet stretched on for a couple of minutes. He'd said his piece, and now he had to give her time to mull it over. It was a lot and she'd been doing a great job so far, dealing with everything life was throwing at her.

He checked his cell, hoping for a text from Dagger. There was nothing. His cousin Hudson had checked in a couple of times, though. Right. The text messages must have finally gone through. He responded to the last panicked text, stating he was alive and well. *On a mission. C U soon.*

Hudson gave a return 'thumbs up' emoji. At least now his cousin didn't have to stress about Vaughn's whereabouts or wonder if he was all right.

"I'm tired," Katy finally said. "Think it would be okay if I laid down a little while and rested my eyes?"

He had no idea how she would be able to do that after several cups of coffee, but emotional stress was often times the most draining.

"Go for it," he said. Plus, he couldn't exactly promise

she'd be sleeping on a bed every night. Or *any* night once they left this place. He wasn't kidding about taking it one moment at a time earlier. That was how missions went in his unit overseas. Always on the ready. Always ready for a fistfight or gunfight. Being on the ready was the only way to survive.

Katy got up from the table, rinsed out her mug, and then moved to the loveseat where she curled into a ball.

Vaughn checked his phone again before reminding himself a watched pot never boils. He was eager to give Katy a little piece of good news for a change, rather than pile on more stress like it felt so far.

The least he could do was place a cover over her to keep her warm. By the time he double-checked the rucksack to make certain all the necessary supplies were packed, and found a light blanket, she was asleep. He covered her before returning to the table. For a hot minute, he thought about trying to power nap as well. The rest he'd gotten last night should be enough to carry him a few days with a few naps in between.

He grabbed his cell phone and sat on the floor next to where she slept. There was something comforting about being this close to her. She brought out his protective instincts and, if he was being totally honest, more than a few good memories.

Katy was a big part of his past. There was so much of him and his happiness during high school that related to her. In so many ways, they'd grown up together. They'd spent their formative years together and he owed a lot of his current maturity to the steadiness of their relationship when his own home life had been messy.

And he still remembered the first time she walked into ninth-grade Biology class after summer break. It was the strangest thing, because they'd gone to the same middle and elementary schools. They'd been in the same tag groups. In different tag groups. They'd played against each other in dodgeball during PE class. But the minute she stepped into the room on the first day of high school, first period, he'd noticed her. He'd been smitten in a serious case of puppy love that blossomed into something he'd believed was real between them.

Even now, he tried to chalk it all up to raging hormones that made him have a physical reaction to her that was beyond anything he'd experienced since. As a grown man who'd been in his fair share of relationships, someone should have come close by now. Granted, first loves were always the deepest. They occurred at a time when neither party knew what a shattered heart felt like. There was an innocence to it all when they didn't realize how devastating a breakup was going to be.

Now, he didn't go there with anyone. Years passed by and he believed he was broken, incapable of feelings anywhere close to those he'd experienced. He chalked the change in him up to growing up, being an adult. He tried to substitute great sex for real connection.

Since he was overthinking everything about his dating life, or lack thereof recently, he acknowledged that he was in trouble when it came to being around Katy. She stirred emotions in his chest that he believed were long since buried.

Maybe this was a good thing. Maybe it was time to think about finding someone to settle down with. Maybe it was time to give up on trying to replace what he'd had with her.

He glanced out the window. It was snowing. The only thing he hated more than spiders was snow.

~

Katy woke to Vaughn's voice. He was gently shaking her, but the look on his face when she opened her eyes said she needed to wake up urgently. She pushed up to sitting. "What's wrong?"

"We have to go," he said. "Now."

Those words were the equivalent of a bucket of ice water being thrown on her. He held a hand out toward her, so she took it to help get to her feet faster. Her shoes were waiting right there. He took a knee and helped her slip into them.

She noticed he was dressed and ready, coat on. Meanwhile, she'd been sound asleep and hadn't heard a thing.

"It's cold outside," he said, helping her slip her arms into a coat. "You'll need this." There were gloves too, so she put those on next. At least they had appropriate clothing for the weather.

Questions mounted as to what was happening but there was no time to ask. Vaughn shouldered the oversized backpack that had been sitting next to the desk that had been moved. An escape hatch was open where flooring should be. She followed him toward it.

"I'll go first and wait for you at the bottom," he said. "Count to ten and then follow me. Okay?"

"Will do," she said.

He gave a thumbs up sign before dropping into the hole. One. Two. Three. Four. Five. Six. Seven. Eight. Nine. Ten.

Katy held on a second longer as her feet dangled into the dark hole. She squeezed her eyes shut before taking the leap of faith. After the launch, she opened them again. The metal was cold on her bottom as the coat rode up her back on the slide.

Only a few seconds passed before she was dropped onto

the grass. Vaughn immediately helped her up, linked their fingers, and made a beeline for the trees. Her heart battered the inside of her ribcage and her thighs burned at this pace. She knew better than to question it, so she pushed harder, doing her best to keep up, whereas he wasn't even breaking a sweat.

He turned his head enough to say, "We have a few seconds before Dobermans will be chomping at us from behind. I don't know what else is coming but it won't be good."

"Got it," she managed to get out through labored breaths.

At this rate, it didn't take long to reach a fence on the back of the yard.

"It's live, so don't touch it," he warned, looking up at trees, no doubt trying to find a way across without getting barbecued. He moved close to the fence and cupped his hands. "I'm going to help you get over."

The fence itself was only five feet tall if she had to venture a guess. The fact that it was hotwired meant it didn't need to be any higher to stop most of what would come through here, which she assumed was dangerous animals. Then again, the most dangerous animal was probably man.

Katy put her hands on Vaughn's shoulders, nervous about the plan to toss her over. He was strong. She didn't doubt his abilities. Could she manage not to fry herself on the way over?

Placing her foot inside his cupped hands, she locked onto his gaze. A moment of doubt nearly paralyzed her.

"You got this," was all he said. Those words shouldn't bring the comfort they did. His faith in her meant the world. "On three." He studied her.

"Okay," she replied.

"One. Two. Three."

Before she could launch a last-minute protest, she was flying over the fence. When she landed safely, albeit in a thud on her side, she exhaled and ran a visual scan to make sure she'd made it over in one piece. The backpack followed a few seconds later.

And then her gaze flew to figure out how Vaughn was going to make it over without assistance. To make matters worse, the sound of dogs barking in the not too far away distance sent her blood pressure flying.

Vaughn backed away from the fence until he was out of view. And then she heard the thunder of his footsteps as he approached in a dead run. His face twisted in determination and concentration as he pumped his arms, and an almost inaudible grunt tore from his throat as he launched himself into the air.

9

Vaughn coiled his legs, hoping like hell that he'd clear the fence with both feet. It was cutting it close. Under normal circumstances, he wouldn't worry. He could jump like a freakin' gazelle. But he was working with an injury and, therefore, wasn't at full capacity, so this was a gamble he had no choice but to take.

It paid off as he tucked and rolled with the landing.

There was no time to congratulate himself, so he reached for Katy's hand. She met him halfway.

The second he had her hand secured firmly inside his, he bolted. The motorcycle should be approximately a football field away from this location. Since he'd played the sport growing up, he had a good handle on just how far that was and how long it should take him to reach the dirt bike.

The temperature had dropped as snowflakes floated down from the sky. Heavy clouds filled the sky. He had no idea where he was going to take Katy or how he was going to keep her warm. He hadn't gotten that far yet since he'd dozed off back at the apartment, much to his surprise. Falling asleep was a sign of trust neither could afford considering the skills of the men who'd been chasing them. Vaughn had kept the two of them a step ahead of the enemy, not exactly a comfortable lead.

The motorcycle was exactly where he'd been told it would be. Thank heaven for small miracles. The way his life was going lately, he wouldn't have been surprised if it had been stolen or found by whoever caused Psycho to sound the alarm. He'd warned Vaughn about the heat on the place, so this didn't necessarily mean R.S.'s people had found them.

He grabbed the helmet, and then handed it over to Katy. "Here. Put this on. It'll help keep you warm, in addition to offering some protection."

She took it and immediately strapped it on. Next, he shifted the rucksack to her so she could hold tight against his body. She'd been on the back of a dirt bike with him plenty of times during high school. More of those memories surfaced when she climbed on behind him and wrapped her arms around him, locking her hands together in front of his heart.

He'd already retrieved the key from underneath the front tire, so he started the engine and followed along the side of the mountain. It was flatter here, which made traversing the terrain a whole lot easier.

Glancing in the rearview, his second stroke of luck came when no one followed.

The frigid air was enough to wake him up that he didn't need a jolt of caffeine, a lot of good that had done earlier.

Staying at the apartment had almost been too good to be true. The warm, cozy place felt more like a fever dream at this point. At least they'd had a chance to rest, refuel, and shower. They had supplies now that they didn't have before. Supplies that could help them fly under the radar for a few more days while he figured out a plan. If her uncle had that much time. R.S.'s intentions remained to be seen.

Would bringing him out and parading him around as bait draw more unwanted attention?

Vaughn shelved the thought for now. There was no use spinning out over it anyway when he needed to focus on their immediate problem. Shelter. At this temperature, there was no way they could sleep outside.

Could he find a garage?

The map he'd studied while at the apartment before Katy woke up indicated a small town was just over the mountain. Then, there wasn't much besides highway for a long stretch. They would have no choice but to hide in plain sight. If the folks who'd raided Psycho's place weren't after Vaughn and Katy, that shouldn't be too much of a problem.

A motel room was probably asking too much. By now, folks would be looking out for the driver of a minivan. Although, according to the news, the person was missing somewhere in the woods. The official story was that the driver and passenger must have gotten into an argument that ended with a crash and murder. The law had no idea who they were looking for. There was no description to work from, and the person driving the minivan was believed to still be wandering around on the mountain, injured and possibly dead.

The manhunt would be contained to the area hours east of their current location, which was another compelling reason to continue west. He didn't like getting farther away from Texas, though.

Vaughn was rethinking the motel idea. Getting Katy inside a warm room would be nice. Of course, they could slip inside someone's garage easily enough. Body heat would keep them warm. Any shelter that kept them out of the wind would be welcomed.

Twenty minutes went by quickly while he was mulling over options. If Dagger didn't come up with something soon, they would have no choice but to return to Texas. The reality that they would have to anyway wasn't lost on him, as much as he would like to keep her far away from anywhere she might be vulnerable. Her uncle was in danger. Telling her to stay away from him when he needed her after he'd been her saving grace as a kid wasn't something that would go over well.

Vaughn stopped and cut off the bike's engine.

"We'll have to walk from here," he said, taking the rucksack from her. He tucked the keys underneath the front tire and set the helmet down next to the bike.

"What happened back there?" Katy asked. He realized she was behind the eight ball since she'd been asleep when Psycho had broken everything down for Vaughn if he needed an exit plan. The knowledge had come in handy. It wasn't the first time a safehouse had been raided and wouldn't be the last.

A wind gust cut right through his coat. She shivered.

"Let's find a place out of the cold first," he said. "I'll explain everything then. Okay?"

"Sounds like a plan," she said. Her teeth were already chattering.

Vaughn wrapped an arm around her as they headed toward the small town. For one, it would keep her warmer. Secondly, it would make them look like a couple in love. Since she'd taken her purse with her and left nothing behind in the minivan, the news said the law was looking for any information about a driver.

Since minivans were common family vehicles, most

folks didn't even notice them as they drove by, especially if there was a man and woman seated in front. The cover seemed to be working so far since the news was trolling for information, meaning they had nothing to go on. A call went out to notify the sheriff if anyone knew anything.

A blacked-out house with a detached garage got his attention. They circled around, checking for vehicles. There was a truck and a boat parked inside the two-car garage. The boat would keep them up off the concrete.

"Stay right here," Vaughn said before disappearing around the front of the home. He checked the mailbox. It was full to the point of almost overflowing. The homeowners looked to be out of town.

He wouldn't risk it by staying in the house. But the garage would keep them out of the wind, and the boat would keep them off the floor where heat would be leached from their bodies.

Katy was right where he left her, but he noticed she'd taken off one of her gloves and palmed a rock. He took note not to underestimate her. She was a firecracker underneath all that beauty. She also seemed poised and ready, despite her fear.

He jiggled the door handle on the side of the garage. She fished out a bobby pin and then handed it over. It didn't take long to pop the lock once he'd straightened the pin.

"Do I want to know why you're so good at that?" she whispered as he cracked the door open. Homes were often wired with security alarms. Garages weren't usually included, especially when they were detached. This time was no different. He twisted the locking mechanism after closing the door behind them.

"Probably not," he said quietly.

The fishing boat wasn't huge, but it offered bench seating.

"Climb up," he said after offering a hand up. She removed her other glove, took his hand, and then climbed aboard.

He looked around the garage, and located a thick, old blanket folded up on a shelf. It was probably used to lay down on when tinkering in the garage and would do the trick nicely to keep them warm.

"I left everything back at the apartment," she said as though she was finally able to think clearly for the first time since being on the run again. "My purse. My cell. Everything."

"They're inside my rucksack," he said.

"Rucksack?" she parroted. "I'd call it an oversized backpack."

"That's essentially what it is," he said. "But I threw everything inside the minute I got the call from Psycho to vacate."

"That's a relief," she said on a sigh.

"Stand up for a second," he said before opening the blanket all the way. He positioned it so that he could fold it in half like a sleeping bag. "There you go."

"That's much better," she said. It offered a little buffer against the cold seat.

He sat next to her, and she immediately cuddled up next to him. The rock had been placed to the side, no doubt for easy access in case she felt the need to use it. He took out his Swiss army knife. "Take this. It's more effective at killing someone than a rock."

Hearing how that sounded as it came out of his mouth, he apologized for his bluntness. "I've been in the army so long, that I sometimes forget how something like that might sound to a civilian."

"It has to be hard to adjust back and forth," she said, taking the knife and setting it next to the rock.

"This is the first time I've come home," he admitted, much to a shocked-looking Katy.

⁂

KATY HAD questions about his military record, but she knew better than to ask. Most of the information was probably classified anyway. "Why *are* you here, by the way?"

"Your uncle called asking for a huge favor and so I took emergency leave," he said.

"Why would you do that?" she asked. He clearly didn't want to be around her for a second longer than he had to, especially when he'd first shown up. He hadn't bothered to hide his disdain for her.

"Because he asked and I had the time to give," he admitted, pulling the covers over them while urging her to lie down.

"I'm the last person you wanted to see again, Vaughn. Admit it."

"That's not completely true," he said. "I would never have accepted the mission if I couldn't stand the sight of you. Besides, part of me wondered if you ended up working in Dallas like you'd always planned, for that nonprofit that puts on the Cattleman's Ball."

"Cattle Baron's Ball, you mean," she corrected.

"Right," he said. "I knew it was something like that."

"The answer is no," she said. "I never made it to Dallas. Made it to Fort Worth, though. Worked a few auctions, organizing sale items and doing project management work to pull everything together."

"Relationships?" he asked, surprising her with the question.

"I've had a few," she admitted. "Nothing worth talking about, though. I just haven't been focused on it."

"What type of work do you do now?" he asked.

"Project management for different fundraisers," she said. "It's a virtual job, which I like. The pay isn't so great, but I make ends meet and I figure it'll lead to something good eventually."

"Sounds like important work," he said. Once again surprising her.

"I've been part of raising funds for orphans and battered women," she said with a warm smile. "The work is amazing. Hours are long, but I don't really mind when it's for a good cause."

"You always did have a big heart," he said with something that sounded a lot like a hint of pride.

"Thank you, Vaughn," she said quietly. "That means a lot coming from you."

"We used to be close, remember?" he asked before adding, "maybe not as close as I thought we were, but close nonetheless."

"You were the only person I let in," she said. "So, yes, you weren't just a boyfriend to me. You were my best friend."

He nodded and got quiet for a long moment like he did when he was contemplating life back in the day.

"I wish you would have felt comfortable enough to tell me everything you were going through, Katy. I would have done things a whole lot differently."

"I know that now," she said. "But I just wasn't ready at the time. I didn't know how to talk about it, so I just stuffed everything down deep and pretended like my life was normal."

"This might sound strange, but I think I understand," he said with compassion that threatened to shred her defenses. She couldn't afford to allow it because being with Vaughn reminded her of everything she had been missing in life. "You were a child and didn't really know what you were doing."

Could she open up a little bit more to him without feeling like she was bearing her soul?

This was hard. Life was hard. Being honest was hard.

Katy took in a deep breath. "Thank you. It's strange to think about it now, but I just didn't believe anyone could understand what I was going through. You were a child too. And neither one of us should ever had had to be put in that situation. Plus, you had your own issues to deal with, so I didn't want to add to that. Especially when it was easier to get lost in your arms when we were together and pretend real life wasn't actually happening. It probably sounds like twisted logic, but I embraced it back then."

"To be honest, I think you were more mature than most back in high school," he said. "Which is probably what threw me off so much when you…"

"We should definitely talk about something else," she said, unwilling and unable to relive that painful memory. They couldn't go back and change the past. They didn't have a future. Not together. No matter how drawn to him she found herself, she was still that girl who couldn't truly trust anyone and he was still that boy who needed freedom.

"Why do you always change the subject or close up when things get difficult?" he asked, shocking her with his brutal honesty.

10

Vaughn was probably pushing too hard, but dammit, he needed answers.

"I guess I didn't realize that's what I was doing," Katy said defensively. She'd been positioned in the crook of his arm but shifted the minute the truly hard questions came out. It was par for the course with her. When facing anything difficult, she retreated.

"I shouldn't have called you out like that," he said, offering a way out. She'd opened up more than any time in their long history. He needed to back off because she was like a wounded animal when cornered as he put her on the spot.

Katy sighed. "You're fine. It's fine. Everything is fine."

Those weren't the words of someone who was 'fine.' Experience had taught him that wasn't the word he wanted to hear during a disagreement with the opposite sex. "Hey. Look. We don't have to go there. It's cool. But let's not go backwards. Okay?"

"What do you mean by that?" she asked.

"We covered a lot of ground and made progress here," he said. "I would hate to wind back the clock. That's all."

Katy was silent for a long moment. He expected her to be regrouping so she could come up with an appropriate argument. Instead, she blew out a breath. "I'd like it if we could move forward instead of looking back, let alone go back. As hard as these last few days have been, I can't imagine doing any of this with anyone but you, Vaughn."

Her vulnerability came through as she spoke. It was hard as hell to stay mad at her when she was practically opening a vein. Talking had never been her forte. Serious conversations sent her running. Looking back, he realized how few times they'd talked about anything other than plans for their futures or how hard an upcoming test was going to be. He also realized he'd done most of the talking, which was saying a lot from someone who wasn't known for being chatty. There'd been a lot of hanging out and kissing. They were a typical high school couple. Although, nothing felt average about the way he felt for her. Those intense feelings were a little too easy to recall now. It was almost like they'd been lying dormant, waiting for her to come back into his life to remind him of how it truly felt to be in love with someone.

He gave himself a mental headshake.

"No looking back," he said, unsure he could keep his word. "Or at least that's the goal."

"I'll take that deal," she said with a whole lot of enthusiasm.

"You know, not everything was bad in the past," he pointed out. "We had a lot of great memories together and it would be a shame to forget those." Was he speaking for a party of one? "At least I did."

Katy didn't immediately speak. He didn't need to look at

her to know she was chewing on the inside of her cheek right now. "Being with you was the only bright spot in my high school days, and it was like I had a bright, warm personal sun shining on me. It scared me too."

"Doesn't sound like something to be afraid of to me," he said. Given her abusive past, he wondered if her parents' relationship played a role in her fears.

His cell buzzed, cutting into the moment. He fished it out of his pocket, sat up, and checked the screen. "Help yourself to food in the bag while I take this."

She nodded as he answered.

"Hey, tell me you have good news," he said to Dagger.

"I wish I did," Dagger said. "This is about the boys who were in jail."

Vaughn took note of the use of past tense. "Did they escape? Make bail?"

"Not exactly," Dagger hedged. "They were found hanging in their cells an hour ago. It's being billed as a double suicide."

"Damn," Vaughn said. "That means this R.S. person either has connections inside the law enforcement community, or these guys were so afraid of retaliation they took their own lives. Either way, this is bad."

"Yes, it is," Dagger said. "I thought you should know."

"We can't show our faces to law enforcement or be connected in any way to this," Vaughn reasoned. "But I wish I could go down and interview the sheriff responsible for keeping his inmates safe to feel him out and see if he's involved."

"That would be Shane Wilcox," Dagger said. "I did a little digging into his background, and he came up clean. I'll stay on it, though, and check out all his deputies."

"I'd start with the one on duty at the time," Vaughn said.

"Already on it," Dagger informed. "Turns out that's not so easy to determine, because the person who was supposed to work that day switched shifts with somebody, and no paperwork was filed. At least that's the story I'm being told."

Vaughn had a feeling his buddy would have already thought through the easier moves and covered those bases. This mission had become a chess game. The right moves and countermoves would determine the winner.

"Do you think it's a larger scale cover-up?" Vaughn had to ask.

"No. It's a small department that sounds disorganized and like this happens so often no one really takes note," he said. "I'll figure it out if I have to hack into their damn security cameras."

"Sounds like that'll take a little longer," Vaughn noted.

"Not if I get lucky," Dagger said, never one to shy away from tooting his own horn.

"Thanks for the update, man," Vaughn said.

"Maybe next time I'll have better news, or at the very least a lead," Dagger said.

The two exchanged goodbyes before ending the call.

"I caught part of that conversation," Katy said, sitting up and eating a power bar. She handed one over to Vaughn. When he took it, their fingers grazed, causing more of that electricity to shoot through his arm. It also reminded him of what had been missing from physical contact with others. He'd had chemistry with the women he'd dated. There had to be a physical attraction for him to want to spend one-on-one time with someone. There'd been less in the way of laughter. Katy was intelligence and beauty, combined with a sharp sense of humor that got to him every time.

Being reminded of all the things he'd loved about her wasn't a bad thing. This was telling him what to look for in his next relationship. After being with her, he was reminded not to settle for less than what the two of them had shared because it had been special.

Vaughn could see himself locking down with someone who made him feel again.

He'd taken the mission, in part, to get closure so he could move on from Katy. He'd been unsure what to expect when he found her. And now, he got what he came for.

Once this mission was over, he could think about taking the next step in his life and finding someone who made him want to stay home on a Saturday night, instead of going out with his unit to party. One-night stands had never held any appeal to him. There had to be enough chemistry and interest for him to want to wake up next to the person more than once. He might not have been offering his heart but he'd found a few people he enjoyed being with enough to have a brief relationship.

Vaughn brought Katy up to speed on the jail situation. The lost look in her eyes returned when she heard the death count that was racking up.

"I feel like we're paddling hard to keep our heads above water here without making any progress toward shore," she said on an exhale. "There has to be something else we can do besides hide out and wait for other people to do the heavy lifting."

"Patience wins battles," he said.

The same logic applied to life circumstances,..and maybe to love?

~

Sitting here, doing nothing, caused Katy's mind to spin

out. "I need a distraction. Too many awful thoughts are fighting their way into my brain."

"How about this," Vaughn started. "Let's see." He paused while he took a bite and then chewed on the opened power bar. "Remember that time you opened your locker and it exploded with glitter freshman year?"

"That was you?" she asked, slapping at his arm like she'd done so many times in high school.

"It was my way of flirting with you," he said. "But you got so mad there was no way that I was owning up to it."

"Billy Banks got detention for that," she said. "You let someone else be punished for something you did?"

"Do you know how many times he got away with stuff and blamed it on other people?" he asked.

"Fair point," she conceded. "Still. I was picking glitter out of my hair for a week. Even washing it every night barely made a dent. It was in my clothes *and* my eyelashes, by the way."

"Yeah, sorry about that," he said. "It seemed like a good way to get your attention at the time."

"Oh, it got my attention all right," she said, taking a deep breath. Vaughn had a way of lightening the mood by picking just the right story to tell. "Was that you who tied my shoelaces together underneath my desk when I was taking a math test in eighth grade?"

He shook his head. "I didn't really notice you until ninth grade."

She couldn't help but laugh. "That's nice."

"I didn't mean it to sound like that," he seemed to catch how that sounded. "Some other guy must have had a crush on you in eighth grade. I didn't notice you until the first day of high school in Biology class."

"We went to school together our whole lives," she said.

"What do you mean you didn't 'notice' me? We played on the same tag groups for heaven's sake."

"Sure, when I saw you as a buddy," he said. "Then you changed. Or, maybe, my eyes finally started working."

"I got my braces off that summer," she said. "I guess I grew into my height. Started filling out. My uncle..." She heard her own voice crack on the word *uncle*. "He took me to Dallas to go shopping for school clothes. My parents weren't good about doing that for me even though we had enough money. They both worked." She felt the mood drop at the mention of her parents and decided the subject was off limits for the time being. She shrugged. "I guess I just finally grew into my long limbs." She didn't look up while she was feeling vulnerable. "You, on the other hand, shot up like crazy. You were still growing."

"I can't say that I was ever skinny," he said on a chuckle. "My football coach had us conditioning too much for that."

"No," she said. "You were always solid." Muscled with looks that caused most high school girls' hearts to flutter every time he walked into the room. Funny enough, he never seemed to notice. Or maybe he just didn't care. "Any other pranks that I should know about now that we're apparently playing truth or dare?"

"I stopped after the glitter fail," he said. "You probably don't remember, but I asked you out for coffee shortly after."

"Oh, I remember all right," she said. "You were personally responsible for my white chocolate mocha addiction in high school. Now, I look back and think about all the sugar intake and what that must have done to my body."

"All those hormones probably required that much caffeine and sugar to stay operational," he said, stretching out those long legs. "I remember being tired all the time."

"You were still growing," she said. "Of course, you were

exhausted. Plus, you worked the ranch alongside your cousin. How is Hudson, by the way?"

"He's good," Vaughn replied. "Getting married, with a kid on the way. Anise was pregnant when they met. They had a whirlwind courtship apparently. I'm not completely caught up on family goings-on."

"As I remember correctly, you used to distance yourself from just about everyone but Hudson," she said, realizing his family life was almost as complicated as hers had been. He'd come to school with the occasional black eye, blaming it on football practice if a teacher asked. She suspected he'd gotten into it with one of his brothers or cousins. He didn't talk about his mother and father all that much and kept her shielded from them even back in the day. When she visited him on the ranch, the two of them were always outside or in the barn. He never wanted to go inside the house. They'd take the horses out for a ride. Vaughn had been the epitome of an outdoorsy person. She, on the other hand, generally stayed inside a building. The library was one of her favorite haunts. Studying there offered a predictable quiet. Home was the opposite. She never knew what she'd be walking into there.

"We were always close," he agreed. "It's hard to believe all my cousins are engaged or married and in the process of having families. At least my brothers haven't fallen down that rabbit hole. At least, not that I know of."

"This is the age people start doing those things," she said. "Announcements fill my social media page, which is exactly why I don't visit often."

"You never talked about marriage or kids, now that I think about it," he said. "I just assumed we were on the same page and would plan a future together someday. But now that I look back, we never had an actual discussion."

She shook her head. "I've always been good at avoiding topics that stress me out."

It was surprising how much she'd discussed her family situation with him since they'd reunited. She never talked about her parents, especially not the abuse she'd endured. There was a big part of her that hoped exposing her parents and the hell she'd gone through might help him understand why she'd walked away from him back then. Maybe make him hate her a little bit less for it.

"I can't blame you," he finally said after a thoughtful pause. "I didn't go inside my parents' house until I knew they were already in bed, so I can't say I was better back then. Avoiding them seemed a whole lot easier than facing them. I guess everyone is guilty of that at one point or other in their life."

Her heart danced a little bit at the admission. A second chance, this time as friends, was probably too much to ask for. She would take forgiveness if he could go there. Maybe not hate her for the rest of their lives. The worst part of the past eleven years was knowing the person she'd loved never wanted to look at her again. Those were the words he'd said to her moments before she got inside her car and drove away from his family's ranch. Those were the words that replayed in her thoughts when she was curled up on her side at night, hugging her pillow. Crying. Those were the words she'd believed would make being in the same room with him ever again impossible.

Katy was beginning to believe in miracles.

11

Vaughn didn't believe in miracles. He didn't put stock in good luck. He'd never been one to toss a penny in a water fountain to make a wish come true. And yet, he couldn't deny there was some magic at work that brought him into the same room with Katy.

Laughing with her felt good. Being with her felt good. But that good feeling wouldn't last because people rarely changed. Habits were the most difficult things to break whether they were positive or negative. Patterns were even more set. Tactical units spent a fair amount of time watching people's patterns in order to figure out the right time to strike for maximum damage.

Katy wouldn't be able to help herself either. If he opened the door to allow her back inside his heart in any form or fashion, history would repeat itself. For now, he was fine reliving a few good moments from their past. It reminded him of the reason why he'd fallen for her in the first place.

"Who stole the cheese from the cafeteria on pizza day in tenth grade?" she asked. "You must know something. Everyone wanted to be your friend."

He gave her a confused look. "Like who? I don't remember there being a line to hang out with me."

"Please tell me that you weren't that blind in high school," she said, making a face. "And I do believe there was a line of girls wanting to spend time with you. You should have seen all the dirty looks I got when you weren't around."

"You should have said something," he said.

"Like what? Help me beat off the girls who wished they were me?" she quipped. She shook her head and smirked. "I mean, dating you definitely made me less popular."

"I doubt it," he said. "Do you know how many guys walked past me in the locker room after practice and told me to take care of you or they would?"

"No way," she said. Her cheeks turned three shades of red. Embarrassment shouldn't be sexy. Yet, there she was… doing just that, giving it sex appeal. "I promise you're lying."

"I promise that I'm not," he said. "Remember Chase?"

"Your friend," she said. "How could I forget him?"

"Then you recall he dated Leanna for the longest time," he said.

"And broke up with her on many Friday afternoons during football season, only to ask her to be his girlfriend again come Monday morning," she said, twisting her face in disdain. "We all know he cheated on her without 'technically' cheating on her."

"How many times did I try to pull that?" he asked.

"Zero," she said quickly. "I'm not Leanna, though. I wouldn't have taken you back on Monday."

"No," he said on a chuckle. "You wouldn't have. But I was never stupid enough to let you go for a minute, because there would be no going back. You would have had your pick of guys, but I was the lucky bastard you chose to be with."

"That's not exactly how I remember high school, but it sounds like a compliment so I'll take it," she said, smiling.

Making her smile warmed him in the center of his chest.

"It's always funny how we see things from our limited point of view instead of the way they really are sometimes," he said. "If you'd looked up every now and then, you would have seen the way other guys looked at you."

"I didn't need other guys to look at me when I had you," she said.

"Believe me, I appreciate your blindness," he quipped. "If you'd known you had options, I wouldn't have had my weekends full of dates with the most intelligent, funny, and beautiful girl at Lone Star Pass High School."

"We couldn't have that. Now could we?" she teased as her cheeks full-on blushed. The fact she didn't realize those things about herself made her even more interesting. She never would have described herself as any one of those things, except maybe smart. Her grades alone should have told her that she was packing a powerful brain. The years of abuse must have taken a toll on her self-confidence as a kid, which frustrated him even more that he'd been too blind to see what was going on.

His parents had bickered like cats and dogs, which was part of the reason he'd stayed away from home. Jackie Firebrand cared about expensive things, status. He was disappointed more than shocked that she'd gone to the lengths she had to secure an inheritance. It twisted his gut to think she could stoop so low or become so dangerous.

Forcing his thoughts to something less depressing, he said, "I still can't believe you wouldn't let me take you to prom. I thought all girls dreamed about going to school events like that."

"Are you saying my surprise was somehow less because

we didn't have to spend a fortune on wrist flowers and gowns that no one ever wears again?" she quipped.

"Those weren't my words," he defended. "And, no, it wouldn't even come close. I just thought girls liked those traditions. Believe me, no guy I knew wanted to throw on a suit and be chaperoned by the Crank, aka Ms. Carla Cowden, so they didn't stand too close on the dance floor. We weren't even a religious school, but she pulled people apart if they danced too close, saying to leave room for the Holy Spirit."

Katy laughed a real laugh this time.

"But you decorated the back of my truck with those hanging lights," he said.

"Fairy lights," she corrected.

"And you threw down a six-by-six piece of plywood so we could dance however close we wanted," he continued. He stopped at the part about that night being right up there with the best of his life. No one forgot their first time making love. She'd brought a thick picnic blanket to throw on the back of his truck. She'd lit some kind of candle, citronella. It kept the mosquitoes away. And then she'd rocked his world.

"Even though we didn't do a whole lot of dancing that night," she said, the red blush returned to her cheeks, making her even more beautiful if that was even possible.

"That was probably a good thing with my two left feet," he said, trying to crack a joke that didn't quite work. The air charged with electricity. "I'd be stomping all over you with my size fourteen boots."

Of course, those good memories would bring back the rush of feelings they'd experienced all those years ago. At this point, they didn't catch him off guard. They were like a tidal wave he'd caught and had to hold onto his board while he rode it to shore. They had the same out of control feeling that a rogue wave would cause. Best not to overthink any of it.

When this mission was over and Katy could return to her normal life, he would be able to put her behind him. He promised to do just that.

"You were a better dancer than you ever gave yourself credit for," she countered. "In fact, you were good at everything you tried, if memory serves."

"Ask my pre-Cal teacher about me and I'm certain you'll get a very different response," he said.

"Let me correct that to anything you put your mind to," she said. "You hated pre-Cal as I recall."

"Might be the other way around," he joked. "Pre-Cal hated me."

"I don't even know why we had to take the class," she said. "I don't know about you, but I've never needed to use it again. Accounting is a different story when I'm balancing the books after an event. I could have used an actual class in that."

"You don't remember Enterprise City?" he asked.

"The field trip from hell?"

"One could put it that way," he said with a chuckle.

"First of all, I'm pretty sure that happened in fifth grade," she said. "I don't know very many people who were running their own businesses at that age."

"You're still bitter our store outsold your refreshment stand, aren't you?" he teased.

She folded her arms over her chest and faked a decent pout. "Am not."

Vaughn couldn't remember the last time he laughed this much, which was saying a whole lot about where his life had been. He joked around with the guys in his unit, but it wasn't anything like this.

It could be all the memories, but he hadn't felt this human in a long time. His stress levels over the past twenty-four hours had experienced a marked decrease. Those didn't normally lower around anyone. In fact, they usually went the other way.

Shared history was to blame for him lowering his guard around Katy. And now, more than ever, he regretted not going for that kiss.

∼

KATY DROPPED her gaze to her hands. She was twisting her fingers together like she'd always done right before she knew Vaughn was going to kiss her. She balled her fists, then flexed and released a few times to work off some of the tension in her body.

Kissing Vaughn was something she badly wanted to do. He'd been right before to put a stop to it, though. Where could it go besides more pain?

Trust wasn't something a man like Vaughn gave easily. She'd had his at one time. Now? It was gone. He would never give her the chance to break his heart twice. Case in point. His best friend Chase stole a lighter from the grocery store. When an employee cornered him, he said Vaughn had dared him to do it. Chase started crying, and Vaughn had been chewed out and banned from the store for a month. Chase had panicked. It had been a stupid thing to do, and he apologized. Vaughn told him where he could take his apology. He was graphic. That happened junior year and the two still weren't talking at graduation more than a year later. There were no do-overs when it came to Vaughn if he gave you his trust. On the flip side, he was the most loyal person anyone could ever hope to meet. It didn't come easily, but once he gave it to you, it ran deep. The only way to lose him was to break his trust.

"It's good to see you again, Katy," he finally said after a long silence. "The circumstances suck, but this is good."

"I'm probably the last person you ever wanted to speak to again, let alone help," she said. "So, it means a lot to hear you say that and I'm happy to see you again too."

He nodded.

"Besides," she began, needing to lighten the mood again, "you're kind of a badass. I mean, you were always strong and, like, Mr. Football hero, but you actually know how to save my life. That's pretty cool for two kids from Lone Star Pass, Texas."

"We did all right," he said with a smile that released a half dozen butterflies inside her chest. And then he locked onto her gaze. "Can I ask you a question?"

Katy swallowed to ease the dryness in her throat. "Sure."

"Are you happy?" he asked. "I mean *really* happy? Not social media happy where some people paint on a smile and make their lives seem so much better than it really is."

"I'm doing work that I feel is important," she said, not directly answering his question. "That counts for something."

He nodded.

"How about you?" she asked. "Are you happy?"

"I'm proud of everything I've done for my country. I want to go home to the ranch, but I don't know if I fit there anymore," he admitted in a moment of raw honesty. "Hell, I don't know if I fit anywhere anymore."

"How so?" she asked. "Is it because of…the things you've done?"

His lips compressed into a frown at the realization she was talking about the people he'd killed. She had very little experience with the subject and was still reeling from the body count. Seeing a dead person would probably haunt her for years to come and she didn't want anything to do with the clothing she'd left behind. It was clothing she'd witnessed a dead person while wearing. It was a strange sensation. To have watched a person die and not try to save them. It went against all her instincts, despite survival kicking in at that point.

"Believe it or not, it becomes easy to compartmentalize it all," he admitted. "Probably too easy. Unpacking it at some point might catch up to me. Right now, though, I'm successfully avoiding dealing with all the loss of life. Plus, you'd be surprised at how clean your conscience can become when you know you're fighting on the right side." He paused for a few long moments. "I left Lone Star Pass a cattle rancher. Now, I'm something else." He didn't say the word *killer* even though it hung in the air between them. "I knew who I was when I left town and now...not so much."

"I know who you are," she decided to speak up on his behalf if he couldn't. "From what I've seen so far, not much has changed. You're still the most honorable person I've ever met and probably ever will. You hold true to your word, just like you did all those years ago. You're honest to a fault."

A smile ghosted his lips at that comment.

"You know it's true," she said, nudging him with her elbow.

"There's no reason to speak if you're not telling the truth," he defended.

"Thank you for making my point exactly," she said. "Right on target with that one."

"Doesn't make it less true," he said, but his lips upturned in the corners of his mouth in a sly grin.

"No, but it can make you less popular," she teased. Popularity hadn't been a problem for him in high school, no matter how much he might have deflected the attention. In fact, he seemed happy enough coming over to her house on a Saturday night, watching anime on the computer in her room, while eating popcorn in bed—on top of the covers, per her parents' orders. At least when he was there, they didn't fight. They never did publicly. On the car ride home was a totally different story. Inside their home could be a war zone at times. As long as the neighbors didn't clue in, anything was fair game.

"Some things in life are more important than racking up 'likes' on a social media page," he quipped.

"We are in agreement there," she said. "I've always been bad about posting, but then I think it's good to keep some things about life private. You know? I think there's a lack of privacy now that seems wrong on some level."

"I don't even have any of the apps on my phone," he said. "It's probably a good way to keep up with people you don't see very often. I'm sure some people make friends that way. Call me old fashioned, but I'd rather call someone than send a text, if that tells you how ancient I am."

"We're both about to turn thirty, Vaughn," she pointed out. "I highly doubt that qualifies you as ancient."

"It feels that way sometimes," he said in another raw moment of complete honesty. "Like I'm not from this generation in some ways."

"Believe me when I say that I know exactly how you feel," she said on a sigh. "Texting has its uses, but I'd rather hear someone's voice when we're communicating. You know?"

"My point exactly," he said. "It's more personal that way."

"It's easy to call someone and see their face now too," she said.

"I've seen some of the guys call home that way," he admitted. "It seems to help when they can see their wives' and kids' faces. They say it's a whole lot better than just hearing a voice." He shrugged.

"Don't tell me there hasn't been anyone special in your life, Vaughn."

"Since you? I don't really go there…"

His voice trailed off. There was no accusation in his tone, just a hollow sound that she recognized as similar to the one in hers when she thought about relationships.

This seemed like a bad time to let her heart get away from her, especially with the new knowledge there hadn't been anyone special in Vaughn's life since her. And yet, her heart seemed to have a mind of its own as her pulse picked up speed.

12

Vaughn's cell buzzed. He immediately reached for it, saw there was a text. "It's from Dagger."

"What does it say?" she asked.

Vaughn stared at the screen, taking a second to digest the news before relaying the message. "It has to do with your uncle." He locked gazes with her. "I'm sorry."

Katy's chin quivered before she turned her face away. She sniffled and wiped away what he assumed were a few tears that had spilled down her cheeks. After a deep breath, she faced him again. "What do we need to do to make certain these bastards are locked behind bars for the rest of their lives?"

"We go to your uncle's home and dig around," he said. "The law will be all over the place."

"It's a shame we can't talk to them," she said.

"Are you his only next of kin?" he asked.

"Yes," she said.

"He didn't have a girlfriend or significant other?" he continued when she blinked at him.

"This was all kept a secret because of my uncle's political

career, but I'm surprised you didn't realize he was gay," she stated.

"Oh." The fact Vaughn had never seen the man with a date or heard about a woman he was dating probably should have clued him in. "I just thought he kept his private life to himself."

"Yes," she said. "That's true. But also because it would have been political suicide in his district if word got out all those years ago. Today, it would have been sticky, but he probably could have survived it."

Vaughn nodded. "Well, then you're the next of kin, so the authorities will want to speak to you about your uncle's death."

This was the second best way to draw her out of hiding. Vaughn bit back a curse. He'd just been outmaneuvered. It was time to switch from defense to offense.

They would have to leave here sooner than he'd like.

"Your uncle lived in Fort Worth, but he had an apartment in Austin as I recall," Vaughn said.

"He 'technically' lived in Fort Worth, yes. But he spent ninety-nine percent of his time in Austin," she said, tilting her head to one side. The blank look on her face said she'd tucked her feelings down deep. He understood. It was the only way to keep moving forward. At some point, those would bubble up to the surface. He was just as bad about doing the same thing. It was the only way to march ahead when he'd had to take a life.

He was also starting to realize he'd been using the same coping mechanism for most of his life. It got him through the day and let him sleep at night for the most part.

"The Austin apartment is where he would most likely keep his personal belongings," he said.

She nodded.

"He showed me a safe once. It was a long time ago," she said. "It's hidden underneath the flooring in the master closet of all places. The thing is indestructible."

"Then we definitely have to start there," he said. Getting them to the apartment alive was his job. "I need the address." He handed over his phone after pulling up the map feature.

Katy typed the information into the cell. The address was to a luxury three-bedroom apartment with views of the capital building.

"He loved being able to walk outside his apartment to a coffee shop," she said. There was a wistful quality to her tone. With a big family like his, he couldn't imagine losing everyone. As messed up as his family could be, he should be thankful he had one. The bottom line was that he knew he could call Hudson or most of his brothers or cousins if he needed help. He and Rafe had some patching up to do, Vaughn had to believe the two of them could figure it out over a beer. Vaughn and his family might disagree on most everything in life, but he had to believe they would step up to help each other if push came to shove. Granted, not all of them got along but someone would take the lead. There would be a few who would rally together and come to his aid.

Speaking of family, he hadn't checked in on his father since the arrest. Kiefer Firebrand hadn't been much of a father, but their shared DNA should mean something. Vaughn needed to check on the man. Being on another continent had made it easy to turn his back on everything going on in Texas. It was time to go home, fix his mistakes, and figure out if he still belonged in Lone Star Pass once he finished out his time in the military.

Vaughn studied the map, memorizing the streets. He

virtually 'walked' them for the next hour and a half, familiarizing himself with alleys and building exits. It was amazing, and probably dangerous, just how much could be researched about a location online without ever setting foot in a place.

The dirt bike wouldn't get them far. He needed a vehicle. Hell, an airplane would be nice...

Hold on. One of his buddies bragged about having twenty-four/seven access to a plane, along with a pilot's license. They'd teased him to no end, and he'd ended up with the nickname Wingman because he was married and vowed not to cheat on his wife, a vow he'd lived up to.

He pulled up Wingman's contact information, then made the call.

"Long time no see, Firebutt," Wingman quipped. Vaughn could have ended up with a worse nickname. His came following a rough bout after eating a ghost pepper on a dare.

"Wingman, whatsssssup?"

"Chillin' over here, but this is your dime," Wingman said.

"I need a ride in the sky," Vaughn said. "I can't tell you the reason and I should warn you there could be danger."

"I'm in," Wingman said. "If I have to run carpool one more time, I might lose it. I'm in a fight to be first in line with a brown Honda Odyssey, and I've already lost twice this week." He released a string of expletives that would make his grandmother roll over in her grave.

Vaughn couldn't help but laugh. He would love to witness Wingman battling it out with another parent for who gets to be first in line to pick up their kids. He still hadn't adjusted to the thought of the man being a father. Like Katy mentioned, this was the age for marriage and family. "Not exactly rocking the adrenaline rush on that one, are you?"

"You know how competitive I can be," Wingman said.

"And how bad tempered you can be when you lose," Vaughn quipped. He recalled the time they lost two Monopoly pieces because Wingman pulled a 'clear the table' move after he lost Park Place, forcing a monopoly with Boardwalk. A month later, the vacuum cleaner found one and the other one seemed to go the way of a disappearing sock in the dryer.

"We don't need to talk about that, man," Wingman joked.

"I appreciate your willingness to drop everything," Vaughn said on a serious note.

"Where are you?" Wingman asked.

Vaughn took a screenshot of his current location and then texted it.

"I know where that is," Wingman said. "Give me till 0600 and meet me at Boulder Municipal."

"Got it," Vaughn said. He set up a ride with a vehicle-sharing service under a fake account. The pickup was confirmed for 0500.

Katy sat quietly as he put pieces in play.

"We should try to get some rest," he said to her. "It'll be a long day tomorrow, and who knows when we'll get a chance to sleep again."

"I can lie down, but I'm not sure that I'll be able to sleep," she admitted as he looked into those gorgeous blue eyes. The urge to kiss her was a physical ache.

"Remember when you asked about a kiss?"

"Yes," she said, dropped her gaze to her fingers that were twisting together.

"Is the offer still on the table?" he asked.

She slicked her tongue across her bottom lip, leaving a silky trail. "Yes."

The one word was all the incentive he needed to close the gap between them and claim those pink lips.

~

The second Vaughn's mouth came down on Katy's, she felt like she'd finally found home again. Getting too used to it would be a mistake, but she wanted this more than she wanted air and wasn't afraid to go with her heart instead of logic. Consequences be damned. And there would be consequences.

The feel of his thick lips as they covered hers sent warmth swirling low in her belly. A half dozen butterflies released in her chest when he brought his hands up to cup her face, and then deepened the kiss. She parted her lips for him and teased his tongue inside her mouth.

He tasted earthy and sweet, like the honey almond power bar he'd eaten. Those would be her two favorite flavors from now on.

Katy brought her hands up to anchor herself, digging her fingers into his shoulders as their breath quickened and her body heated. She'd never experienced a kiss so intense or with so much promise. No one had come close to the feelings she'd had when they'd kissed in high school either. The grown-up version of the two of them was beyond anything she could have ever imagined.

Sex with Vaughn now would be life-altering. It would set a new bar for what intimacy should feel like. It would bring a release that only he could give her. But would it be a mistake? Those words disintegrated faster than sugar in hot tea the minute he dropped his hands to her thighs and urged her toward him.

She climbed on his lap, breaking apart for the briefest few seconds, her thighs wrapped around him. There was only two layers of denim in between them. She could feel his stiff length pressed against her inner thigh as his big hands with those long fingers wrapped around either side of her hips.

Their breaths were coming in rasps as she dug her fingers deeper into his shoulders to anchor herself against the coil tightening inside her, building, begging for more. She bit down on his bottom lip and teased it between her teeth. His tongue plunged inside her mouth the second she released his lip. He pulled back, teasing the tip in until she stood on the edge of the point of no return.

Much more of this and she wouldn't be able to stop.

Pulling on every ounce of willpower left inside her, she pushed off his shoulders and sat back on her heels, shifting off his lap. Their breathing labored, she couldn't help but crack a smile.

"Damn," was all she could manage to say.

"Damn is right," he responded with a dry crack of a smile in return as he tried to catch his breath. It was like they'd just crossed the finish line of a 5k.

"Thank you," she said. "I needed that." She needed to be reminded that she was still alive. She needed to be reminded that she was capable of experiencing that kind of all-consuming passion. And she needed to be reminded there was a beating heart inside her chest. One that very much wanted to be able to let go of fears and insecurities so she could trust.

"Believe me when I say I'm the one who should be thanking you," he said, taking her hand in his. She resisted the instinct to pull back. Instead, she let herself feel comforted by his touch.

"Let's agree this kiss was mutually beneficial," she said, feeling a lightheartedness that she knew wouldn't last. They were facing a serious enemy, who at the moment, was unknown. Their ability to hide their identity gave them an advantage.

"Done," he said, bringing her hand up to his lips before brushing them against her skin so tenderly her heart skipped a few beats. More of those butterflies launched.

She lived in the moment, stretching it out as long as possible, not wanting to let go of it.

Reality loomed.

"What are you thinking about?" he asked.

"How do you know when I'm distracted?" she asked.

"Your eyes get a blank look, like you've gone inside yourself, and you get a tiny wrinkle across your forehead," he said. "Same as in high school."

"Oh, right," she said. The outside world blurred when she started thinking deeply about a topic.

"Is it something you can talk to me about?" he asked. The pad of his thumb drew circles on palm. The rhythm was sensual and comforting at the same time.

"It's selfish, because my favorite family member in the world just died and I'm wondering if that means I'll never get an answer to the question of paternity," she admitted, more than a little ashamed.

"Wanting to know who your parents are isn't selfish," he countered. "It's reasonable."

"What if he knew and that information dies with him?" she asked before adding, "I can't even begin to process the fact he's gone."

"It gets easier to stick those feelings in a box and tuck

them down somewhere you hope you never find again, doesn't it?" he asked with a wistful quality to his voice—a voice that was now low and gravelly. It stirred places inside her that she believed were tucked away in one of those boxes.

"Yes," she answered anyway. "But what happens when there's no more space or the boxes run out?"

"In the end, you hope that never happens," he admitted. She appreciated that he wasn't trying to solve her problems so much as let her know that he not only understood but felt the same way. Much like her, he didn't have the answers.

"Surprisingly, talking about it to you actually helps," she said.

"Why does that surprise you?" he asked with a hint of disappointment in his tone.

"It shouldn't, except that we didn't leave on the best of terms years ago," she said. "My fault." She added those words quickly because she didn't want him to think she blamed him in any way, shape, or form. "I just can't imagine talking to anyone else about something so personal. So, I've kept a lot bottled up inside to the point my chest hurts when I breathe some days."

"This might come as a shock to you, but I like the fact you can talk to me," he said. His thumb, the connection, the rhythm, soothed her.

"Good," was all she could manage to get out.

Being with him now made her realize just how much she'd missed him. If they lived beyond this mission, could they be friends?

13

Vaughn opened the covers enough for Katy to climb inside. He joined her and she immediately scooted over next to him, molding her body to his when he put his arm around her. She positioned herself in the crook of his arm where she fit him to a T.

"We'll need to be awake in a few hours," he said, realizing they'd talked until midnight. "Even if you can't sleep, power down for as long as you can."

"Okay," she said in that soft, sleepy voice that she somehow made sexy. It tugged at his heartstrings and stirred up a whole lot of conflicting feelings.

Right now, though, his laser focus had to be on finishing the mission with them both alive. She would need to swing by Austin PD to speak to the chief. Lawmakers had deep ties. Hopefully, the police department could be trusted. Small-town sheriffs were a tossup. Some were good at their jobs and took it seriously. Others got the job because of their connections. Those could be scary. Lucky for Vaughn, he'd kept on the right side of the law during his youth, so he didn't have to find out what he was working with in his county. He'd heard from Hudson that Timothy Lawler was doing a good job. The sheriff had been a legend on the football field. Vaughn had heard stories despite being quite a bit younger than Lawler. He'd been a star quarterback in a state that took the sport about as seriously as anyone could. The story went that Lawler was being scouted by some big name programs when he took a hit that broke his arm in four places. The high school senior at the time had still managed to get off the game-winning throw, but the injury had ended his career and any hopes of playing college ball.

Lawler wasn't who they would be dealing with. The chief was an unknown. Vaughn reached for his cell phone and fired off a text to Dagger to ask for anything he could find out about the chief. A politician being killed on his watch would be a nightmare for the chief. He would stay involved in the case even though it was made to look like he drowned in Barton Springs.

This could be a setup. An accidental drowning in a story that builds to reveal his sexuality. It sickened Vaughn to think this man's private life could be used to try and tarnish his reputation.

After sending the text, he glanced down at Katy. Her long blonde hair splayed across his bicep. Her steady, even breathing said she was asleep. It took a lot of trust to fall asleep with someone under these conditions. He wasn't exactly a stranger, but he took her trust as a compliment anyway.

Vaughn went over the map in his head over the next few hours. At 0400, he eased out from underneath the covers and then walked the garage. He grabbed supplies and then slipped out to check the perimeter. While there, he brushed his teeth, shivering in the cold as he spit into the woods.

By the time he returned, it was time to wake Katy. For a

few seconds, though, he stood next to her and watched her sleep. She looked so peaceful that it was almost a shame he had to wake her.

"Hey," he whispered, not wanting to startle her.

She blinked those blues open, stretched her arms out, and smiled. All he could say was that his heart was going to take some damage when he walked away from her this time.

It didn't take but a few seconds for her to register their surroundings. The smile faded as reality dawned.

She sat up and rubbed her eyes. "What time is it?"

"A little after four," he supplied. "Thought you might want a little time to gather yourself. There's a good spot to brush your teeth behind the garage." He wanted to leave as little DNA behind as he could. The snow would help wash away their spit as it melted. Plus, there was no reason for anyone to swab back there. They would be gone and out of here without leaving a trace in the next forty-five minutes.

He had no idea when the homeowners would return but they had no reason to suspect anyone had broken into their garage.

Katy slipped out of the covers, grabbed supplies, and threw her coat on.

"Do you want me to come with you?" he asked.

"I got this," she said.

He nodded, took out alcohol wipes from the rucksack, and proceeded to erase the fingerprints from the boat and garage. By the time she returned a few minutes later, he was finished and the rucksack was sitting beside the door where he stood waiting for her. He'd folded the blanket and returned it to its spot.

"The car is almost here," he informed. "Your name is Alice and mine is Jacob. We're a couple who've been visiting friends."

"Shouldn't we have luggage?" she asked.

"This will make it believable." He shouldered the rucksack.

"All right then," she said. "Should we be waiting out front on the porch?"

"We'll be okay back here. I instructed the driver to pull up out front and he'll believe there's a guesthouse back here. He won't question us," he said.

"You have it all figured out," she said with a hint of awe in her voice. "Sounds pretty thorough."

"Details are my specialty," he said with a smile, trying to keep things light for as long as possible. The day would get heavier as they returned to Texas and she had to face her uncle's apartment. He hoped the information she needed would be inside the safe. While he was wishing, he hoped the person behind the initials was discovered.

"Before the driver gets here," she started, reaching for his hand. "You told me my uncle...but you didn't say what happened to him."

"Drowned while swimming in Barton Creek," he said. "It's been written off as an accidental drowning."

"My uncle was afraid of water," she said, shaking her head. "He would never have gone in willingly."

Good to know. He glanced at his phone.

"The driver's almost here," he said, taking note of her revelation and the sadness in her eyes with the news. "Let's head out."

She nodded and then surprised him by pushing up to her tiptoes and pressing a kiss to his lips.

No words were needed for them both to know they were in dangerous territory on a personal level. Except he suspected this kiss was her way of telling him that she cared, just in case they didn't survive the day. He intended to prove to her that he could keep her alive.

It was an unspoken promise he intended to keep.

∽

Playing newlyweds, Katy wrapped her arms around Vaughn's waist and snuggled as close as she could while they walked. He had one arm around her, holding her close. The body heat was welcomed against the bitterly cold morning.

The heat was on inside the small sport utility.

"How are the roads?" Vaughn asked the driver.

"Not bad," the driver said as Katy clicked on her seatbelt, before burrowing into Vaughn's side.

The drive to the small airport took a little over half an hour. Vaughn peppered sweet kisses on her forehead, jaw, and lips a few times along the way. She figured it was a good way to keep the driver from staring at them.

Vaughn thanked the man before making a show of rating him after exiting the vehicle. Ratings went both ways with drivers and passengers. There was a not-so-subtle suggestion to leave a tip, which Vaughn did.

A thought struck Katy as they walked toward the sliding glass doors of the small airport. She stopped cold. "I'm the only heir to whatever money and property my Uncle Blaine owns. Won't that automatically make me a suspect in his death?"

"Not as it's currently being ruled an accident," he said. "But we'll keep an eye on the situation."

She thought about lawyers and court dates. Arrests. It was hard to believe this situation could possibly get worse. A frigid wind blasted her as a stocky man walked outside to greet them, who she assumed would be Wingman. His ear-to-ear grin as he set eyes on Vaughn told her that she was right.

"Long time no see," he said to Vaughn before the pair embraced in what could only be referred to as a bear hug.

"I see you managed to get uglier with age," Vaughn quipped. Wingman laughed.

"Dude, I got out last year. It's been twelve months. I wouldn't exactly call that aging," Wingman shot back. He turned toward Katy, and then made a face at Vaughn like recognition dawned. Why would he know who she was?

She made a mental note to ask Vaughn about it later when they were alone.

"No introductions needed," Wingman said. "The less I know, the better."

She nodded.

"Good to meet you, though," he said before taking them over to his Cessna. All she knew about the airplane was that it had a prop engine.

Vaughn helped her climb onto the wing and then into the backseat, where she buckled up.

"You have good timing, Firebutt," Wingman said. "The weather is clearing up. We should have a smooth flight."

Katy suppressed a laugh at the nickname.

She tried not to think about how many people died in small planes a year. Or how easy it would be to crash. She wasn't a big fan of flying but could rally when she needed to. There was some comfort in how well Vaughn...*Firebutt*... knew Wingman, which was probably a strange notion at best. That he somehow wouldn't crash the plane because the two of them knew each other wasn't a rational thought.

"I can get you into Million Air, south of Austin," Wingman said.

"Sounds good," Vaughn agreed, before reaching back to pat her on the knee from his bucket seat. She grabbed his hand and held on for a few seconds before releasing it.

Wingman was several inches shorter than Vaughn with sandy blond hair and cobalt blue eyes. He had a medium build and wore dark blue overalls and a bomber jacket with several patches down the sleeve. It reminded her of a Boy Scout, but that's where the similarities ended. No matter how easy his smile might be, she had no doubt he was deadly. There was a look in their eyes that was different from civilians, and a way they carried themselves that said they were ready for anything.

It was hard to imagine this guy packing juice boxes and running a carpool. Then again, he sure looked happy. Could someone like Vaughn be happy with a family? With a few kids running around? The image of them as a family with a couple of their own kiddos running around should probably shock the hell out of her. She shoved the thought as far back in her mind as possible.

Maybe it was the fact she'd lost her uncle, her only family connection, that had her suddenly wondering what it would be like to be married with children. It had never crossed her mind as a possibility before.

Now, she thought it might not be the worst thing that could happen to a person.

She could scarcely imagine a world without Uncle Blaine in it. He'd been her rock. It was Uncle Blaine who bought her first cell phone. He'd already programmed his number in the contacts. She'd stayed with him for two weeks every summer, which had been the best of experiences. Uncle Blaine knew all the best coffee shops and restaurants in Austin. Hands down, he was the coolest uncle. She'd overheard him defending her to her parents a few times.

A rogue tear escaped thinking about Uncle Blaine. There was a hole in her chest the size of Palo Duro Canyon at the thought of never being able to talk to him again. He'd been her sanity when she walked away from Vaughn, despite the fact that she'd firmly shut down his questions as to why she'd left.

More of those tears spilled out of her eyes. She crouched down in the seat and turned her face toward the window. Katy was so not a crier, so these waterworks caught her off guard. At least she could see out into the darkness as the plane took off. She didn't feel claustrophobic with all the windows around her, so that was good.

More tears came. She did her best to hide them from Vaughn, but figured she failed because he reached back for her hand and just held it. There was something incredibly powerful about having someone sit with her and hold her hand when it felt like her world was crumbling around her.

By the time they reached Million Air airport, the sun was up and the cabin was warm. The cold front in Colorado must have stalled out west because it looked to be a beautiful morning in Austin. The noise from the prop engine plane drowned out her occasional sniffles as she watched the roads begin to fill with traffic. People going to jobs. Coming home from work. For reasons she couldn't explain, she felt angry. How could the world go on when she'd just lost one of the most important people in her life? It seemed wrong that when her world tilted on its axis everyone else just kept doing what they always did.

Katy took in a deep breath. She'd let herself go to a melancholy place when she needed to focus. Because the next body that turned up dead could very well be hers, with the people behind her uncle's murder after her. And she was one hundred percent certain he'd been murdered.

Setting her emotions aside was the only way she could keep going. So, she did what she was good at and compartmentalized her feelings. Consequences be damned. And there would be ramifications. Could she survive this time?

14

Vaughn noticed Katy wasn't doing well on the flight. He'd never felt so helpless in all his life. He wished there was some way to make everything better, but she'd lost the only family she had left, and his heart ached for her. There were no replacements when it came to loss. There was only heartache and finding a way to live through it until breathing didn't hurt as much.

Holding her hand could only provide so much comfort. She held tight on the descent. He realized that he didn't know everything about her because she was clearly afraid of flying. Was her fear contained to small aircraft or all aviation? He hadn't asked her before making arrangements and felt responsible for her current state of panic.

Since she didn't speak up beforehand, he realized she would do whatever was necessary to get back to Texas. Going all in to accomplish a task even if it meant keeping blinders on was a sentiment that he understood a little too well.

Wingman landed and pulled up next to a building that resembled a small mall. "I'll drop you guys off here."

"I can't thank you enough—"

"You would do it for me in a heartbeat," Wingman interrupted. "No thanks necessary."

"I appreciate it anyway," Vaughn stated. "And you're right. If you ever need an excuse to leave carpool, call me."

Wingman laughed.

"You'll be the first to know," he said.

As Vaughn opened the door and Katy unbuckled the seatbelt, Wingman leaned closer. "She seems like a good one, man. If I were you, I wouldn't let her go this time."

Vaughn didn't have a good handle on how he felt or what he had to offer, so he forced a smile.

The minute his shoes hit the pavement, he turned to help Katy hop off the wing. He felt her body trembling underneath his fingers. Instead of letting go, he brought her into an embrace. Body flush with his, he wanted to whisper all kinds of promises into her ear.

Shoving those thoughts aside as she stepped back, he waved goodbye to Wingman after shouldering the rucksack and walked toward the glass and white metal building that looked like a miniature shopping mall. The vehicle he'd ordered from one of those car borrowing apps would be waiting in the parking lot. The key fob would be underneath the driver's seat, the door unlocked.

"Firebutt?" she asked as they approached the building.

"I'd rather not talk about it," he said, shaking his head and trying to hide being mortified. "But I'll definitely wring Wingman's neck the next time I see him for mentioning it." He shouldn't be surprised his buddy brought it up, considering they all teased each other on an almost nonstop basis. Vaughn would get his revenge at the right day and time.

He located the two-door white sedan, and then opened the door for Katy before coming around to the driver's side, tossing the rucksack in the back, and claiming his seat. He reached underneath the seat and felt around for the key fob. Found it.

His cell buzzed. He fished it out of his pocket and then checked the screen. "It's Dagger." He answered.

"I have eyes on the ground near the address you sent me last night," Dagger started right in. "There are two guys patrolling, both come across as ex-military. One has a Texas drawl and the other is Cajun."

"Damn," Vaughn said. "They must have gone straight there after yesterday's encounter."

"Meaning whoever is behind this has significant financial resources and connections," Vaughn noted.

"My thoughts exactly," Dagger said. "But then a senator is dead, so I figured we were up against something like this."

Vaughn agreed. "You have a description?"

"I can do better than that," Dagger said. "I just sent pictures."

"You are *the* man," Vaughn said.

"Don't forget it," Dagger joked. "That's all I got for now. I'll be in touch when I get more."

"Sounds like a plan," Vaughn stated before the call ended. He pulled up the text and tilted the screen so Katy could see. "These are the bastards who tried to kill us on the mountain."

"That's my uncle's parking lot," she said. "There's his sports car."

She pointed to a canary yellow Chevy Camaro.

"The person who hired these guys must want limited involvement with anyone else. Why else would he send these two all over the place?" Vaughn mentioned, thinking out loud.

"You make a good point," she agreed. "He could have

limited resources, but I suspect these are the only two he trusts."

"Easier to clean up after if this thing goes FUBAR," he said.

"That's true," she admitted. "The Raker brothers suddenly hung themselves in their jail cells. If you believe that's a suicide pact, I have a bridge I'd like to sell you sight unseen."

"My thoughts as well," he confirmed. "We should head that way and get the lay of the land. We have visuals now on who we need to avoid, so that's huge."

"Especially since they know who we are," she said. She looked out the passenger window as he started the vehicle. He pulled up the address on his cell's GPS, and then exited the parking lot. Then came, "I see myself sitting outside on the rooftop deck of a hotel overlooking the capital building tonight. My shoes are off, my feet are kicked up, and I'm having the best glass of sparkling water I've ever tasted."

"Visualizing?" he asked but it was a rhetorical question. His chest swelled with something that looked a whole lot like pride. "Good for you."

"What are you doing later?" she asked, tilting her head to one side.

Telling her the first thought that came to mind probably wasn't a good idea. It involved him, her, and soft sheets.

"Having a beer while sitting with you, I hope," he said.

She smiled.

"The lights at night will be so beautiful," she continued. "What kind of beer? What's your favorite?"

"Blue Moon in a glass with an orange slice inside," he said. "The colder, the better."

"Sounds good," she agreed.

The rest of the ride was spent in companionable silence.

He could almost taste that Blue Moon, but to be honest, he'd trade it any day for the taste of her sweet lips. The kisses they'd shared had imprinted his soul.

Downtown traffic in Austin remained constant. Meaning, there was constant traffic in downtown Austin. The kind that slowed to a crawl and had no rush hour. Every hour was rush hour there. The loop they'd built around the city should have eased some of it, but the city planners couldn't keep up with the influx of folks relocating there. Austin was one of the fastest growing cities in America, topping the list year after year. It had been that way since Vaughn was a kid, and only seemed to get worse in the past few years based on everything he'd heard. Experiencing it proved the news was on point.

He exited I-35 near Hancock Recreation Center and stayed on the service road until he passed the law school. He took the next underpass and came upon Oakwood Cemetery. He stayed on MLK, passing a couple of coffee shops, and then circled the block of a newer apartment building.

"Uncle Blaine lives...*lived*," she corrected, "on the thirty-second floor. He moved to this building almost eight years ago."

"It doesn't look that old," he said.

"The management team takes good care of it. They're picky about who they rent to," she said. "You have to make a certain amount to qualify because the rent is astronomical."

"I remember when folks used to talk about Austin as a bargain place to live compared to other big cities in Texas," he said.

Things changed. Could people? Or was this a case of wishful thinking on his part?

∼

Katy made herself as small as possible in the front seat as Vaughn circled the block. The pair of men were still there, sitting in an SUV with blacked-out windows that were rolled down. There were no cops here. At least none that were visible. She had no idea if any were walking around undercover. The apartment building had a whopping forty-eight floors. Her uncle lived on the thirty-second. His view of the capital was stunning.

"I have a spare key," she said. "Once we get inside the building, there's no problem getting into his apartment."

Vaughn nodded, keeping his gaze intent on their surroundings as he pulled over to the side of the road in a loading zone. Traffic was thick, as always, making it a little easier to blend into the background. Downtown Austin was noisy too. The temperature was much warmer here than on the mountain. She'd figured as much. Any cold front that came through usually blew past fairly quickly. The past couple of winters had been extra intense. Storms stuck around for days, knocking out power and stranding folks without heat.

"There's a back entrance through the pool gate on the other side of the street," she said. "There's no parking, except on the street with meters, but good luck finding an open one."

"Let's check it out," he said, pulling into traffic. He navigated around the one-way streets, zig-zagged through vehicles and nabbed a spot on their third circle.

"You have a new superpower," she said, relieved they could find something so quickly.

"I can't ever count on good luck but it sure is nice when it smiles on me," he said with a hint of satisfaction.

"We're rowing in the same boat on that one," she agreed.

"Would be nice if it was more dependable, but I'll take what I can get."

"It'll play better if we keep up the couple routine," he said.

"It's easier to hide that way too," she pointed out. "You cover most of me when you put your arm around me."

He nodded. "Plus, people look away if a couple seems too lovey-dovey."

"You have my consent to pour it on," she said, before realizing how that might have come across. "I'm not suggesting anything outside of—"

"I didn't take offense," he quickly said. Too quickly? Were his feelings toward Katy changing? She wrote the notion off as wishful thinking.

"At least I don't need winter gloves and a heavy coat," she said. "This sweater will be warm enough."

Vaughn exited the vehicle after pocketing the key fob. He came around to her side and then opened the door for her. Taking his hand sent a wave of sensual shivers racing through her body. She was getting used to her body's reaction to him, drawing a surprising amount of comfort in its predictability.

With his arm around her, they walked into the pool entrance from the street. The world seemed to work off key fobs these days, and Uncle Blaine had given her this one, along with the key, years ago. She'd never been allowed to drive on highways. Austin traffic would have stressed her out way too much, so she ended up flying in and taking a car service when she visited if he couldn't pick her up in Lone Star Pass.

He never discussed much about his partners and he never introduced her to any of them. His private life had always been just that...private. Maybe she'd learned to compartmentalize from him.

They made it inside the building and to the appropriate elevators without drawing unwanted attention. She pushed the button for 32. His apartment was 3207. She stared as the buttons light up. First 2, then 3, then 4. Her anxiety climbed with it, because she couldn't be certain there was no one inside his apartment. It would be a risky move on their part but she couldn't rule it out.

Not the mention how awful it was about to be to walk inside her uncle's apartment knowing she would never see him again. A rogue tear leaked, sliding down her cheek. Vaughn instantly turned toward her and then thumbed it away. Without speaking, without needing to, he brought her into another embrace.

He dipped his head until his mouth was so close to her ear she could feel his breath, and said, "This is probably one of the most difficult things you'll ever do. Your uncle meant a lot to you and I know you miss him. It's not a consolation, but I'm right here. I'm not going anywhere except here. And I'll hold your hand the whole way if that's what you'd like."

He dropped his arm and found her hand. Palm to palm, tingles of electricity pulsed up her arm.

"Thank you," she said. "And I got this."

She'd been so busy thinking about the two men in the SUV that her feelings crept up on her, catching her off guard. Taking in a fortifying breath, she reminded herself that she'd survived a whole helluva lot. As difficult as walking into his apartment was going to be, she had this.

There was no doubt in her mind.

The elevator dinged as it reached the 32nd floor. She'd made this trip dozens of times over the years. All she had to do was put one foot in front of the other. She dug around in her purse for her small keyring. There were four keys on it. She located the match for apartment 3207 as they approached the door. There was a punch code system too, but Uncle Blaine changed it often enough that he told her the master key was more reliable. That way, she wouldn't have to keep up with the new codes.

Everything looked normal in the hallway so far. There were security cameras everywhere. Since she'd come in via the pool gate, she'd managed to skip the front desk. Plus, security knew her here. Her uncle had made certain of the fact. No one would think twice about her being in the building.

Standing at the door, she listened for any sign someone was inside. It was quiet, so she unlocked the door and then slowly opened it.

The apartment was just as she remembered. High ceilings. Wall of windows. Open concept. Modern furniture that somehow managed to be inviting to sit down on. Leave it to Uncle Blaine and his impeccable taste. The good part was that it didn't appear anyone had been inside.

As she stepped over the threshold, memories assaulted her. She had to set them aside for now and get down to business. Vaughn entered right behind her, then closed and locked the door, a stark reminder of how dangerous it was to be here.

Katy made a beeline to the master, which was to the left of the living room. There were two bedrooms on the other side of the kitchen; a guestroom and a bedroom turned office. Her uncle had remarked that home offices were the first place criminals searched. They usually had all the credit card information, home loan, social security cards right in one place. Easy peasy.

Which was also the reason he kept his most important

papers inside the master bedroom safe. Technically, the closet but she wasn't one to split hairs. Now, she just had to remember the number to open it.

Katy dropped down to her knees in the walk-in closet. She peeled back the carpet from the corner to reveal a couple of planks. Those were removed next. She stared down at the punch pad.

"I can't remember the damn numbers," she said.

"Try his birthday," Vaughn offered.

She did. No luck.

"With passwords, a lot of folks use a pattern," he said. "Try running down one column and up the next starting with the number one."

She did. Same result.

Vaughn sat back on his heels. He ran through a lot of possibilities in his head before proposing the next one. "Try your birthday."

"Mine?" Katy asked.

"Yes," he said. "It's worth a shot."

Katy wasn't so sure, but it wasn't like the computer where she would get locked out. She entered the digits. The lock clicked. She grabbed the handle, and the metal door opened right up.

15

The writing was on the wall. It seemed to be clicking for Katy too. Vaughn sat back on his heels as she picked through papers until she found an envelope with her name on it. She locked gazes with Vaughn for just a few seconds but communicated a host of emotions. Fear and anticipation stood out the most.

"This might be it," she said. "It's addressed to me. Maybe he always figured I'd come asking. Maybe it's my birth certificate."

Vaughn noticed she was doing a lot of guessing rather than opening the envelope to find out once and for all. "This could also be a will or his final wishes."

She flicked the envelope. "It's too thin. There isn't much more than a couple pieces of paper in here at best."

He conceded her point.

With a deep breath in and then released, she said, "Here goes nothing."

She ripped open the envelope, leaving zagged edges on the paper. There were two pieces of paper inside. The first was a handwritten letter signed by her uncle. The next was a birth certificate, like she'd hoped.

One look at her birth record and her jaw almost dropped to the carpet. "How is this even possible?"

Vaughn leaned forward and saw the name Blaine Cargill.

"There's no way," she said. "My uncle is and always has been gay. Physically, this is impossible."

"Just because your uncle came out as gay to you doesn't mean he wasn't in the closet at some point in his life," Vaughn pointed out. "You know how difficult it must have been for him considering he hid the fact from the public and even me. I knew him better than many and I didn't have a clue."

She nodded. "He talked about it with me sometimes. My grandparents would have disowned him when they were alive, so he wouldn't even let himself go there." Shock didn't even begin to cover the look on her face. "I believed my mother cheated on my 'dad' all these years. How could I have been so wrong about everything?"

"First of all, you were young and everyone hid the truth from you," he said. "Why would anyone question the people they believed were their parents? Plus, you resembled your mother." He caught himself. "Technically, your aunt."

"Yes, but still," she said. "I feel like I should have known something was up."

"Read the note," he said, motioning toward the handwritten letter. "Plus, you never felt like you had a relationship with your so-called dad. I'd say you had a lot of reservations about being close to him."

She picked it up and started, "Dearest Katy, I can only imagine how you must be feeling right now if you're reading this. It took me years to finally be able to write it, but I wanted to every day. I wanted to tell you the truth so many times but was afraid of the life I could offer. Watching you grow up has been my greatest joy. Getting to witness it after your birth mother wanted to put you up for adoption is something I'm the proudest of. It's not your mother's fault. I dated women for a long time thinking that I could be 'normal' like everyone else and not disappoint my parents. None of this is anyone else's fault but mine. We lost your mother before you went into kindergarten but she had been contacting me, asking about you. My sister banned Layla from seeing you, saying it would only confuse you. Since she'd been the one to take you in and raise you as her own, I didn't feel like I had a right to make demands. Looking back, I have so many regrets. Having you is not one of them. You are the best thing I ever did in this life and I hope you know how much I wanted you. I didn't earn the right to call myself your dad, so I won't do that now. All I can ask is that you can look into your heart to see if there's any way you can forgive me for all the years of lying. I never wanted to hurt you. Love, Uncle Blaine."

Tears rolled down Katy's face as she set the letter down. She picked up the birth certificate and read her mother's name out loud. "Layla Winters."

"It's a beautiful name," he said. A corner peeked out from the corner of the envelope. He grabbed the bottom and shook. A picture fell out of a beautiful blonde woman who must have been Layla. "I think this might be her."

Katy picked up the photograph, studied it.

"She looks like me," she finally said. "Or maybe it should be the other way around."

"There is definitely a resemblance," he said.

"My mind is spinning right now, but this explains a lot," she said. "There are so many pieces clicking together and I know that I should probably be mad but I'm relieved the man I believed my father my entire life wasn't."

"I'll never understand how someone can hurt an innocent child," he stated through gritted teeth. "And I understand it even less when you created that person."

"I wish my uncle would have been strong enough to tell me sooner," she said. "He might not think he deserved to be called Dad but I do. He was so much better to me than the man who raised me."

"I'm guessing that he must not have realized Mark was hurting you physically," Vaughn said.

She shook her head. "He would never have allowed that to continue, and I was good at hiding the evidence. You'd be surprised what a little makeup can do to cover bruises."

The muscles in Vaughn's shoulders involuntarily tensed.

"It's possible your 'parents' couldn't conceive, and this seemed like a good solution for everyone," he surmised. "I can only imagine bringing up children is one of the hardest things in the world. Maybe the man who raised you didn't think it through long-term."

"I always knew he resented my uncle because I preferred to stay with him," she said. "Now I know why."

Since they didn't need to stay inside here any longer than absolutely necessary, he said, "We should gather up anything that looks important and get out of here before anyone notices."

"Right," she said, peering down into two-by-two feet safe again. "My uncle had a gun in here."

"Wouldn't do much good in there if someone broke in the apartment," he said.

"The master bedroom door is solid, and it locks, just in case of trouble," she supplied. "I locked myself in once by accident and he panicked. I was twenty-one, so it was fine. He was always overprotective."

The look of relief in her eyes spoke volumes. It was important for people to know where they came from.

"At some point, I'm going to have to have a minute to myself. Because I need to slow down and process everything," she said. It was probably good that she hadn't had the chance yet. Emotions had a way of stacking up on a person and once the floodgates opened, it was damn near impossible to stop the tidal wave from flowing.

"I'd be happy to provide privacy for you when this is all over, but I'm hoping you don't mean on a permanent basis," he said, surprising himself with the admission. Right now, though, he had to maintain focus on keeping her safe. The papers in her hands might get them closer to finding out who R.S. was. Justice was all he could think about right now.

The snick of a lock sounded in the next room. Vaughn grabbed Katy's hand and led her back into the bedroom where she stuffed the papers underneath the mattress.

"Hello," a male voice called out. "Katy?"

She shot a look at Vaughn that said she had no idea who the voice belonged to. He reclaimed her hand before glancing around to see if there was a watch or something she could pick up. He pointed to his wrist and she nodded before moving to the dresser and opening the top drawer. She pulled out an expensive-looking Swiss watch and held it in her hand.

"Answer," he whispered.

"In here," she said, heading toward the living room with Vaughn right behind her. She met the owner of the voice halfway down the hall. He froze the second he got a look at Vaughn.

"Are you *his* Katy?" the sandy-blond-haired man asked. He was tall and tan with a runner's build.

"I'm Bobby," the sandy-blond-haired stranger said expectantly as though she should automatically know what that meant. He frowned when recognition didn't dawn on Katy. "I worked on the Hill with your uncle."

Co-workers could explain why Bobby had his own key. Of course, there was another, more plausible reason that Katy wasn't cluing into.

"We were special friends," Bobby said. "I'm at a loss without him." The man looked ready to break down.

"I'm sorry," Katy said. "And I'm sorry that my uncle never introduced us."

"He never even spoke to you about me?" Bobby asked.

"I'm afraid not," Katy came back honestly. "But he never included me in that part of his life, so I hope you're not too offended."

"He kept secrets," Bobby finally conceded. "Sucks that we had to hide from everyone. I'm out, so that made it even more difficult on him."

"Can I ask a question?" Vaughn asked.

"Sure," Bobby looked Vaughn up and down with appreciation that was creepy under the circumstances.

"You called out Katy's name," Vaughn started. "How did you know she was here?"

"Security called," he said. "I asked them to inform me if anyone came here and they recognized her."

"Who else might have shown, if you don't mind my asking?" Vaughn said.

"He had a habit of forgetting to get keys from his exes once they broke up," Bobby said. "Once news broke, I figured someone might show."

Vaughn took note of the excuse, not sure he liked the answer.

"I'm sure you'll be going through Blaine's things over the next few days," Bobby said. "This is an awful job. You're welcome to take what you want and then leave the rest to me to clean up." Bobby sniffled as he brought his hands up to cover his face. "I have no idea how I'll box up any of his stuff when it still feels like he might walk through the door any second."

"I'm sorry for your loss," Katy said. "You must have loved each other very much."

Bobby nodded. "He was my best friend. I have no idea how I'm going to go on without him."

Katy felt awful for Bobby. She couldn't imagine losing her soulmate. The irony that she'd found hers when she was too young to realize and then ruined everything wasn't lost on her. Because in eleven years, there should have been someone else she got excited about. Instead, she'd convinced herself that true love was a fantasy, and settled for dating people she liked but could never see herself with long term. She was also starting to see how truly messed up her parents were and that not everyone ended up like them.

Right now, she had to figure out how to get Bobby out of the apartment so they could leave with the papers.

"Do you want something to drink?" he asked. "Tea?"

"We should probably get going, right?" she turned to Vaughn for an answer. They could always come back but this was risky enough already. Getting in the first time might have seemed easy but they'd hit at the right moment and, she'd believed, slipped right past security.

Someone was watching.

The thought creeped her out.

"We have a few minutes, hon," Vaughn said, surprising

her. He urged her toward the kitchen and she realized he was getting them out of the hallway and away from the papers.

∿

"I'll put on a pot of hot water," Bobby said.

"Sounds good," Vaughn said. "Do you have anything stronger?"

"Like vodka?" Bobby asked.

"I was thinking more like coffee," Vaughn responded. He'd redressed the bandages on his thigh, so he was good to go there. Bobby was suspicious. Vaughn could tell by the overly drawn-out emotions. But what was his game?

"Is espresso okay?" Bobby said with a shiver like he was shaking off something gross. "We never kept coffee in the house."

Vaughn picked up on the word *kept*. Bobby might be a gold digger. Was he here to clean out the apartment of any valuables before Katy arrived?

"The watch looks good on you, by the way," Bobby said as he pulled supplies out of the cabinet, and then threw a pod into a machine that sounded a whole lot like they were inside one of those fancy coffee shops when it kicked to life.

"It was one of his favorites," she said.

"I know," Bobby replied. "I bought it for him. Check the inscription."

Katy took off the watch and turned it over.

Love you to the moon and back, B.

It was clear the two were romantic partners. Bobby still had a key to the place but by his own admission Blaine wasn't good about requesting his key back from his exes. Was Bobby one of those exes coming to take what he believed was his? He must have been in a relationship with Blaine fairly recently if Bobby had a good enough rapport with security for them to call when Katy had shown up. Was he worried she would take something valuable that Bobby believed was his?

"You should take it back," she said, handing over the watch.

"No," he exclaimed. "It was a Christmas gift." He put his hands on the white marble counters, fingers splayed. "Besides, he would want you to have it."

"Why is that?" she asked.

"Because he might not have talked about me, but I know all about you," Bobby said on a sigh.

Katy leaned forward. "What did he say?"

"That you were beautiful and smart," Bobby said as the machine spit and sputtered out a very small amount of liquid. He wouldn't believe it would take that long and require *that* much sound to produce so little results.

"He was very sweet and very blind," she said.

"No," Bobby said, pausing for a moment as he studied her. "You look so much like him. It's weird to actually be talking to you, when I've wanted to meet you for so long. Not under these circumstances, obviously."

"It's good to finally meet someone important to my uncle," Katy played along.

Instinct told Vaughn to start checking for exits. On the 32nd floor, the balcony was out as an option. That was definite. He didn't have a belay on him and had no intention of scaling down the side of a building this size.

There were stairs and, of course, an elevator serving this block of apartments.

Bobby turned his back to them for a few seconds to grab the espresso off the machine. Vaughn took the opportunity to make a face at Katy that he hoped she would pick up on. They needed to get that paperwork and get the hell out of there.

She nodded. Good. They were on the same page. Not a whole lot got past her, despite the sympathetic routine. She was good at playing a role. He had to give it to her. She was also very aware of the stakes in this situation.

"Here you go," Bobby said, handing over the small glass cup.

Vaughn downed it in one swallow. The tea would take longer. He feared this was a stall tactic. But why? Had he called the police? Bobby couldn't have been associated with the military guys in the SUV. Could he?

All Vaughn knew for certain was that his gut instinct told him they needed to get out of there. The question was how could they while still taking the papers with them? A second trip wasn't impossible, but it was of concern.

Was Bobby on a fishing expedition? Was he trying to see how much Katy knew? Or was he trying to protect what he believed belonged to him? Courts would give next-of-kin everything in the estate unless Bobby could prove he had a right to take something.

Could he? Or was he fishing around for a will?

The other issue was figuring out a way to get out of there with the documents and doing it fast without raising an eyebrow with Bobby.

16

"Be careful, it's hot."

Katy took the teacup from Bobby, whose hand was shaking. Was he involved in her uncle's murder? She didn't exactly buy the crying act from a few minutes ago. Why wouldn't he send up the bastards in the SUV if that was the case? Why come himself?

The answer dawned on her. Bobby must be looking for something and he thought she might know where it was. No one but her knew about the safe. Her uncle...*father*...had been clear with her that no one else should know.

On that note, so much made sense to her now. She had assumed her uncle had doted on her from a young age because he never planned to have a family of his own. Being lied to for all these years sucked. There were no two ways about it. The reasons behind the lie softened the blow. This was a unique set of circumstances, which made it impossible for her to be too angry. Besides, she was too sad and missed him too much to let herself overthink the deceit.

"How long have you two been a couple?" she asked

Bobby. She didn't doubt the two of them had dated. No question there. He had a key and knew about her.

"Um, let's see," Bobby hedged, looking like he was mentally calculating the dates. "Almost two and a half years now."

"That's a long time," she said, forcing a look of sympathy wasn't difficult considering how close she was to tears since hearing the news about her birth father. "I can't imagine what you're going through losing your partner like that."

"It's difficult," Bobby said, turning on more of the waterworks. He fanned his face with his hand. "I miss him so much already, but my brain hasn't fully accepted that he's not going to walk through that door at any moment."

He was talkative and there was something insincere, almost fake, about his tone.

"It's just so hard to think he'll never put on another pot of tea or snuggle with me on the couch while watching a movie with the fireplace on," Bobby continued.

Was he stalling?

Why?

Was he waiting for the cops to get there? Katy needed to go to the station and speak to the chief. What would Bobby have to gain if she got arrested? But arrested for what? She wasn't in the same state as her un...father when the drowning occurred. Also, her father didn't swim. Strange that his cause of death was deemed an accidental drowning.

"He was such a good swimmer, too," she said, fishing to see how well Bobby knew her father.

"No way," he quickly countered, twisting his face. "He liked to walk near the water, but he never even would have dipped his toe in."

"How could I forget that?" she said.

"You didn't get to spend enough time together," Bobby

countered. He would get no argument there. She wished like anything her father could have been in an environment where he felt comfortable enough to bring her up on his own. "He had to have slipped on the bank and then..."

He flashed eyes at them.

"You know," he said, twisting his hands together.

"Right," she said. "Thinking back, I remember he couldn't even sit on the edge of the pool and watch me swim."

"Exactly," Bobby said. He knew her un...father...well enough to realize he was deathly afraid of swimming. Was there anything else she could test him on?

Better yet, could she grab those documents and get the hell out of there with Vaughn?

"How long are you planning to stay here?" Bobby asked before taking a few deep, dramatic breaths and then picking up his own teacup. He would be considered handsome by most standards. He was easy to talk to. Was this her father's type?

"Here?" she parroted, then shook her head. "As in this apartment?"

"The guestroom has always belonged to you," he said like it was common knowledge. "I just figured you would stay here until you settled up Blaine's affairs."

"Too many memories," she said. "Being here right now is almost too much."

"Oh," he said. "Sure. I guess I can see that."

"In fact, I've probably been here too long as it is," she said. "It gets hard to breathe. You know?" She let herself experience the emotions she'd been barely holding at bay, and didn't turn her face when tears welled in her eyes.

"I do," Bobby said, as Vaughn brought his arm around her shoulders to comfort her. "I'm so sorry for your loss too."

"I'll miss him every day," she said, feeling every bit of that statement in her soul. She would miss his check-in calls that came like clockwork. She would miss having someone who cared about the details of her life. She would miss hearing his voice.

More tears came. She turned toward Vaughn, and cried.

"Do you mind giving us a moment?" Vaughn asked.

"Oh. Certainly," Bobby said. "I'll just be...there's something in my car that I need to grab. I'll be back in a few minutes."

"Thank you," Vaughn said.

Katy's tears were real. Her memories were real. Her emotions were real. Having to shut them down as Bobby slipped out the door was one of the most difficult things she'd ever done. But there was no time. They had to act, and they had to get out of there before Bobby returned.

The minute the lock snicked, she wiped her eyes and mentally shook off the heaviness in her chest.

"Are you okay?" Vaughn asked. "Be honest."

"Well, no," she said. "But this is important and I don't have a choice."

"Okay," Vaughn said. "Let's do this."

In the next second, he was making a beeline toward the master bedroom. She couldn't let her fears take over. Like what if Bobby was listening at the door or walked inside the apartment right now? Instead, she locked in the mental image of her sitting on the rooftop of a hotel with that glass of sparkling water later, adding in the detail of wearing a white cotton robe later.

Vaughn returned around the same time she checked the peephole. There was no one in the hallway that she could see. If Bobby really did, in fact, go to his car was he putting himself in danger of the SUV bastards?

No witnesses. R.S. didn't seem to want to leave anyone behind who could identify him or testify against him.

"Do you think it's possible Bobby knows R.S.?" she whispered as Vaughn joined her.

"Sure, anything's possible at this point," he said, moving in front of her. She realized he was putting himself between her and the door, protecting her just like he had been this entire time. She'd lost a good thing all those years ago. If she could go back and change it, she would in a heartbeat.

Vaughn handed over the papers. Katy's shaky hands let them slip right through. A thud sounded and several of the loose papers went flying, fanning out. She immediately dropped down to her knees and gathered them up.

A name on an envelope caught her attention. Bobby Sullivan. She held up the thin envelope that was sealed. "Look at this."

Vaughn studied the name for a few seconds before taking the envelope from her. "I'll hold onto this one."

The elevator dinged. Katy immediately stood and checked the peephole as her pulse skyrocketed. There was no way Bobby had had time to go all the way down to his car and back. And yet, there he was coming out of the elevator.

It dawned on her that he might live in the building. He tucked something behind his back. Metal glinted against the hallway light with the move, so she assumed the object was a gun. Had he come in without it a few minutes ago to get the lay of the land? See if she was alone? He might have assumed he could take her in a physical matchup. The second his gaze had landed on Vaughn, he'd known the battle was lost. Going hand-to-hand wasn't an option.

"Bobby is short for Robert," she said as Vaughn nodded. He'd figured it out too.

"R.S." he confirmed her suspicion before pulling out his

cell and firing off a text. She could only assume he was giving the information to Dagger, so he could act appropriately.

~

"Hide in the bedroom or office, okay?" Vaughn asked Katy, fully expecting her to put up an argument. It wasn't in her nature to hide. He was asking a lot, but a lot was at stake.

She locked gazes, then nodded before heading toward the master with the papers. It dawned on him that she would want to hide them back in the safe since Bobby didn't know about it. They would be safe inside.

The snick of a lock sounded a few seconds after she disappeared.

Back against the door, Vaughn moved without making a sound. With the door half open, Vaughn made his move. He slammed the door on Bobby to disorient him. In the next second, Vaughn reached around and grabbed a fistful of Bobby's shirt before yanking him inside the room. The door slammed shut as Bobby dropped to the floor, breaking Vaughn's hold.

The guy knew a little bit about martial arts. Vaughn had underestimated Bobby. Wouldn't happen again. Vaugh dove toward the guy, who rolled out of the way just in time. He reached around behind his back, and then produced a pistol. Two seconds later, Vaughn was staring into the barrel of a gun. At this close proximity, missing would be next to impossible even with the worst of shooters.

"Where is she?" Bobby asked, his voice a couple of octaves higher. Fear could do that to a person. Eyes wide, pupils dilated, Bobby was on full-tilt stress mode.

The man was just out of reach or Vaughn would have

kicked the pistol out of his hands—hands that were shaky. Bobby wasn't used to a real fight. Real life was far different than practicing in a martial arts studio.

It was the adrenaline rush that was underestimated by most. It might clear the mind and boost energy, but it also shocked the system and caused someone who wasn't used to handling it to shake as they adjusted to the flood to their nervous system.

Vaughn kip-upped to his feet, then immediately dropped down and swipe-kicked, nailing Bobby in the ribs and elbow. The force was enough to knock the weapon loose. Bobby fought to hold onto it, giving Vaughn the opening he needed to dive into Bobby. He skidded backwards but managed to keep hold of the weapon.

"Freeze or I'll shoot you right now, Bobby," Katy demanded.

Vaughn glanced up in time to see her standing with her feet shoulder width apart, and the gun from the safe aimed at Bobby's face.

The distraction gave Vaughn a chance to knock the weapon out of Bobby's hands. It slammed into the wall, thankfully didn't discharge, before hitting the floor. And then Vaughn got the hell out of the way.

"Put your hands up, you sonofabitch," she said. "Who are you really and why do you know my unc...father?"

"Shoot me and you'll never find out," Bobby said, but there was no conviction in those words. He was trying to cover. The man was so scared Vaughn feared he might urinate on himself. His cover tactics weren't working.

Katy's finger hovered over the trigger mechanism. Vaughn knew what it was like to be forced to take a life. He couldn't let Katy. She might be tough on the outside, but she was covering a tender heart—a heart that had been wounded down deep by her parents early on.

Vaughn shot her a warning look that said to hold off. She gave a slight nod. The look in her eyes said she was determined to do whatever it took to keep them both safe.

"Hands up," she said again, even more sternly this time.

Bobby slowly obeyed. When his hands were safely where Vaughn could see them, he pinned the man down. Tucking Bobby's arms to his sides, Vaughn straddled him, squeezing with his thighs to pin his arms.

"Call the police and give them a description of the men outside," he said to her. "And then call Dagger."

"Blaine owes me this," Bobby said.

"You killed him," Katy said before making the 911 call. "He gave his life. What more could you possibly want?"

"I think you know," Bobby said.

"The protected land deal?" she asked. "You would take a life over a piece of property?"

"You have no idea how valuable that deal is," Bobby said, his face twisting with disgust.

Vaughn drew on all his willpower not to cold cock the guy. He squeezed his thighs a little harder. Bobby grunted.

"You'll have a long time to sit behind bars and think about how much you lost," Katy said after making the call to Dagger.

It didn't take long for the cops to arrive and arrest Bobby along with the pair of unsuspecting men in the lot. Tucked in the backseat of law enforcement vehicles, handcuffed and ready to be taken to jail, the reality was written all over Bobby's face. Justice was going to be served. The papers from the safe were handed over as evidence. And the apartment was empty again.

There was only one thing left for Vaughn to do

17

Katy reached for Vaughn's hand as, one by one, the vehicles left the parking lot. She loved everything about their fingers being linked, the connection she felt when they were, and the reassurance that permeated through her.

Vaughn felt a lot like home.

"It's over," she said to him once they were back in the apartment. "It's finally safe."

Vaughn brought her hand up to his lips and pressed a tender kiss on her knuckle. "Yes."

"Will you stay the night with me?" she asked.

He opened his mouth to speak but was silenced by the sound of his cell buzzing. Vaughn retrieved it, and checked the screen. He looked up at Katy before answering. "It's Dagger."

She could only hope this wasn't more bad news.

"I'm here with Katy," Vaughn said. "I'll put you on speaker."

"Now that I have a name, it was easy to find intel," Dagger said after a perfunctory greeting. "The Sullivan family used to be one of the wealthiest in Austin, but Bobby's father made several bad decisions, so this deal was supposed to put them back on the society pages."

"Why did they target my unc...father?" Katy asked. "Did Bobby know Blaine from living in the same building?"

"The two of them seem to have been closer than that at one time," Dagger informed.

"It's the reason he had a key," she surmised but had already guessed as much. "Bobby said my father always forgot to take back his key once a relationship was over."

"Theirs has been over for months," Dagger said.

The loss of her father was beginning to seed. Katy had no idea what she was going to do without Blaine in her life. Her heart ached, wishing she could talk to him again. There was so much she wanted to say now that she knew the truth. Those words would forever be stored in her heart.

"I'm guessing Bobby thought he could pressure my father into the deal," she continued.

"Blackmail was more like it," Dagger said. "Bobby was threatening to 'out' your father."

The way he called Blaine her father, like it rolled off the tongue so easily, caught her off guard. It also felt right in ways she could scarcely explain. So much about her life clicked into place now. Many puzzle pieces started fitting together.

It would take time to process, but she was happy Blaine turned out to be her parent. She only wished her mother was alive, so she could get to know her.

"Blaine would have done anything to keep the news quiet," she said.

"How did you find all this out so soon?" Vaughn asked, sounding impressed.

"Katy snapped pictures of the documents," Dagger said.

"It's why I was gone so long in the next room," she said. "I was afraid we would lose the information and I would never know what really happened."

The fact Vaughn's chest seemed to swell with pride warmed her heart. Was there any way he could forgive her for the past?

"That was quick thinking," he said. "But then, you always were the smartest one in the room."

She felt a red blush crawl up her neck at the compliment.

"You do all right for yourself," she said quietly.

"The papers will be enough to pin Bobby Sullivan to the crimes," Dagger said after clearing his throat, like he'd just walked in the room and caught the two of them kissing.

"That's all we need," Vaughn said.

"Take care of yourself," Dagger said. "That goes for both of you."

"Will do," Vaughn said. "You do the same."

The call ended after Katy threw in her goodbye. A lump formed in her throat, making it hard to breathe. She let go of Vaughn's hand, needing a clear mind for what she had to say.

After pacing to the kitchen and back, she stopped a few feet in front of Vaughn.

"I have a question," she started, "and it's fine if it's not okay with you for me to ask but I'll always wonder."

"What's the question?" he asked, folding his arms in front of his chest.

Katy took in a deep breath. "Is there any chance you can find it in your heart to forgive me for walking away all those years ago?" She put her hand up. "Before you respond, I'm not asking for anything but forgiveness. I know I hurt you in the worst possible way and I have hated not knowing you for the past eleven years." She brought her gaze up to meet his. "So, is there any chance you'd consider being my friend again?"

Vaughn studied her for a long moment. Her heartbeat thundered in her ears as he took a couple of steps toward her. He closed the distance between them, and then took both of her hands in his.

"I can do a whole lot better than that, Katy," he said. Then, he took a knee. "In all these years, I haven't been able to find a single person who made me feel anything near the kind of feelings I felt for you...*still* feel for you." He looked up at her, locking gazes, and for a man as fierce as him, had the most tender look in his eyes. "I don't think I ever stopped loving you, Katy."

After everything they'd been through, it was almost impossible to believe this moment could be happening right now.

"And I suspect that I'll never love anyone else in the way that I love you," he continued. "So, being friends won't work for me."

She gasped.

"But if you're interested in something else, something deeper, something that has the word 'forever' in it, I'm all in," he said. "Because I love you and I'd be honored if you would agree to marry me someday later on down the road when you're ready."

Katy nodded and smiled as tears streamed down her cheeks.

"I'd marry you right now, Vaughn Firebrand," she said. "I have never loved anyone in the way that I love you. And I want to spend the rest of my life in your arms."

Vaughn stood up before dipping his head down to kiss her.

"That's all I'm asking," he said, his mouth moving against her lips.

"Good, because you're my home."

18

EPILOGUE

Rafe Firebrand's alarm shocked him awake. Squinting with one eye open, he managed to find the snooze button in the dark. The second time the alarm went off had him cursing. Rancher or not, no one should have to get out of bed when it was still dark outside. That went double when it was cold. But Vaughn was back and Rafe needed to find a way to make amends with his brother.

After rolling off the bed and almost face-planting on the hardwood floor, he fired off fifty pushups to get his blood pumping. Normally, his morning ritual was good enough to get the day going. Today was going to be the exception. He bit back a yawn as he clicked the light on and stood up.

Like every morning, he touched the metal picture frame on his nightstand before heading into the bathroom. The five-year anniversary of Emile's death was coming up. The life he'd planned died along with her. Now he was closer to forty than thirty-five with no future prospects and even less desire to replace what he'd lost. Having a family wasn't in the cards for everyone.

A quick shower helped clear some of the cobwebs. Coffee finished the job.

As he walked back to the master bedroom to get dressed, he heard his cell buzzing. It was unusual to get a call this early, maybe it was Vaughn. He picked up the pace. His phone sat on the charger next to his alarm clock.

Unknown number.

Answering would probably annoy him further, so he didn't. Whoever was on the line could leave a message if they wanted a callback. He was already feeling off this morning. Work called on the family ranch he loved and he needed to eat, pack a lunch, and get to the morning meeting in the barn. He'd been second to arrive for two weeks running. His competitive nature had him wanting to beat his cousin Adam, who had the same streak. Who was he kidding? Everyone born with the last name Firebrand had a competitive streak. His grandfather had pitted his two sons against each other, causing a lifelong feud that was finally dissolving. Families were complicated as hell, but this was friendly competition.

No message from the caller. Must be a telemarketer. They were becoming more and more of a nuisance.

The cell almost immediately buzzed again. This company was persistent. This time, he answered the call with a curt greeting.

"Mr. Firebrand, this is Cynthia from EggVault," Cynthia began, and his heart immediately dropped. He hadn't thought about that place in years. A crush of memories sucked the air out of the room.

He grunted an acknowledgment, unable to form words.

"I'm sorry to inform you there's been a mishap in the lab and your wif—"

"Fiancée," he corrected.

"Yes, sir, I see that now," Cynthia continued, her tone solemn. "I'm afraid there's only one vial remaining after a contained fire."

Rafe tried to reach back in his memory to recall what Emile had told him about freezing her eggs. He'd been too consumed with the fact she was dying to care about a future that didn't include her. Now, he wished he'd listened. "What does that mean?"

"Most of the eggs Emile Cassidy had frozen are gone," Cynthia stated. "I'm sorry."

"How many are left?" he asked, unsure what in the hell to do with this information. Should he go ahead and tell her to destroy the remainder?

"Three," she said along with another apology. "According to the file, they belong to you."

Right. The damn file.

"Did she leave instructions?" he asked, remembering how he'd refused to have the discussion about the possibility of her not surviving.

The line was quiet for a few seconds. He reached inside the pocket of his jeans for the lucky mule penny Emile had given him, then remembered it was lost.

"No, sir," Cynthia said. "It just says that you're the point of contact in the event of an emergency."

"That's all?" he asked, his tone a little more heated than intended.

"I'm afraid so," she confirmed. The sympathy in her voice shouldn't annoy him as much as it did. "Take your time in deciding what to do. Call me back when you're ready to discuss."

Rafe issued a sharp sigh before thanking Cynthia for the

courtesy call. It wasn't her fault she had to deliver the news, so he didn't want to take his bad mood out on her.

He took a knee in front of the nightstand with Emile's picture on it. Five years was a long time to be without someone. And yet, in some ways it had gone by in a flash. The love he felt for her was still strong. They'd pledged to build a life together. Three eggs were all he had left of her. Freezing them had been her idea but the move was supposed to be precautionary. She was supposed to live and the two of them were supposed to be married. Freezing eggs was supposed to give them the chance to have a family. Together.

Would she want her child to grow up without a mother? Plus, how would he even go about finding someone willing to…

Hold on a minute. Was he remotely considering any option besides giving the go-ahead to destroy those three eggs?

Smartphone in hand, he looked up the chances three would be enough to ensure a baby would result. The odds weren't just slim, they were almost nonexistent. It would take a miracle.

Rafe stared at the picture of smiling Emile. It had been taken during a trip to the family cabin where they'd spent one of the best weekends of his life. Their relationship was becoming more serious and he'd been nervous as hell. She'd been certain of everything. Of the two of them getting married. Of the two of them having a baby. Of the two of them living to a ripe, old age together. The one thing she'd been wrong about was her own survival.

He absently ran his index finger along the outline of her heart-shaped face, wishing like hell he could ask her what she wanted him to do. Bowing his head, he clenched his back teeth trying to stave off the headache threatening. *Talk to me.*

And then the answer came to him. He knew exactly what Emile would want.

KEEP READING to find out what Rafe does next.

ALSO BY BARB HAN

Texas Firebrand

Rancher to the Rescue

Disarming the Rancher

Rancher under Fire

Rancher on the Line

Undercover with the Rancher

Rancher in Danger

Set-Up with the Rancher

Rancher Under the Gun

Taking Cover with the Rancher

Firebrand Cowboys

VAUGHN: Firebrand Cowboys

RAFE: Firebrand Cowboys

MORGAN: Firebrand Cowboys

Don't Mess With Texas Cowboys

Texas Cowboy's Protection

Texas Cowboy Justice

Texas Cowboy's Honor

Texas Cowboy Daddy

Texas Cowboy's Baby

Texas Cowboy's Bride

Texas Cowboy's Family

Texas Cowboy Sheriff

Texas Cowboy Marshal

Texas Cowboy Lawman

Texas Cowboy Officer

Texas Cowboy K9 Patrol

Cowboys of Cattle Cove

Cowboy Reckoning

Cowboy Cover-up

Cowboy Retribution

Cowboy Judgment

Cowboy Conspiracy

Cowboy Rescue

Cowboy Target

Cowboy Redemption

Cowboy Intrigue

Cowboy Ransom

For more of Barb's books, visit www.BarbHan.com.

ABOUT THE AUTHOR

Barb Han is a USA TODAY and Publisher's Weekly Bestselling Author. Reviewers have called her books "heartfelt" and "exciting."

Barb lives in Texas—her true north—with her adventurous family, a poodle mix, and a spunky rescue who is often referred to as a hot mess. She is the proud owner of too many books (if there is such a thing). When not writing, she can be found exploring new cities, on a mountain either hiking or skiing depending on the season, or swimming in her own backyard.

Sign up for Barb's newsletter at www.BarbHan.com.

Printed in Great Britain
by Amazon